ff

DOMINIC COOPER

Sunrise

faber and faber

LONDON · BOSTON

First published in 1977 by
Chatto and Windus Limited
This revised edition first published in 1986 by
Faber and Faber Limited
3 Queen Square London WC1N 3AU

Photoset by Parker Typesetting Service, Leicester
Printed in Great Britain by
Redwood Burn Limited, Trowbridge, Wiltshire and
bound by Pegasus Bookbinding, Melksham, Wiltshire
All rights reserved

British Library Cataloguing in Publication Data

Cooper, Dominic
Sunrise.
I. Title
823'.914 [F]   PR6053.O5467
ISBN 0-571-13956-6

Library of Congress Cataloging-in-Publication Data

Cooper, Dominic, 1944–
Sunrise.

I. Title.
[PR6053.O5467S8   1986]   823'.914   86–13423
ISBN 0–571–13956–6 (pbk.)

To Dominique, as ever

I should like to thank the Scottish Arts Council
for the bursary awarded to me in 1975
which made the writing of this book possible.

Death, why do you delay? Why are you so slow in coming to me, a man alive but mortal? Why do you not catch hold of him who is longing for you? Who can possibly assess that sweetness which brings an end to all sighing, a beginning to all blessedness, the gate to a desired, unfailing joy? You are the end of my grief, you are the goal of my toil, you are the cause of my fruitfulness, you are the entrance to my joys. Yes, I burn, I pant for you. If you come I will be safe.

Richard Rolle, *The Fire Of Love*

CHAPTER ONE

'Let us pray.'

The light breeze that turned and gently blustered across the small heights of Beinn an Eòin had come from out beyond the open sea. Its movements seemed haphazard and irrelevant in comparison with the ordered lives which the island people followed in the glens below. Its origins and intent were obscure; for it was impelled by a force which drew nothing from the creations of man. And it was only the land with its scarred cheeks of rock and heathers, of fleshy mosses and pliant grasses, only this harrowed mass and the mute but unwavering attention of the distant sun that lay under the wind's progress across the island hills. For the people themselves, drawn away from their old intuitions and unvoiced passions by a new and more rational world, had long turned their faces and were now taken up with matters closer to their lives.

The breeze wandered on over the hill, combing and stroking at the soft surface of the ground, until it came to the lip of an escarpment. There, on the boundary between the two worlds, it gathered itself and sprang high into the thin blue air to form part of a current supporting the buzzards that ran this inland coast in search of food.

From these heights the land below stood in a strangely unreal perspective. Southwards, to the right, the twin coilings of a single-track road and a meandering river emphasized the shape of the glen that was closed by a low pass several miles out of sight behind the hills. Northwards lay the spoonbill shape of a little sea-loch, protected from the ocean surge by the wooded narrows in through which the tides tirelessly raced twice a day. The glen with its slow river met the sea-loch in an encampment of reeds and pools and backwaters; and here, at the head of the loch, lay the clustered spattering of houses which formed the isolated village of Acheninver. From a distance, little or no pattern could be discerned in the arrangement of the buildings and the only prominent feature was the kirk with its squat tower.

Nothing moved. Only the spiralling of the breeze and the occasional cry of a bird marked the relentless passing of the hours. Far below, the village lay pinned flat beneath the rays of the late afternoon sun. Behind the veil of distance, this small human gathering stayed motionless, a fieldmouse in fear of the hawk.

'Let us pray.'

The rustling and shifting died down and in the ensuing silence while the minister gained his composure for the coming prayer, the bleating of a sheep on a nearby hillside carried in through the open doors of the kirk.

In the front pew Murdo Munro glanced sideways at his woman. He looked away again quickly. Behind them the villagers were packed in ranks, men and women alike in their best clothes for the wedding. Shepherds and dairymen, tractormen, foresters, gangers, roadmen, builders and fishermen, their weathered faces creased and scabbed, their eyes polished by the year-long rota of sun and wind and rain, all shifted uncomfortably in their clothes and craned forwards to witness the ritual that would once more bind them closer in among themselves. And the womenfolk, too, gauded up in their coats and perching, flowered hats, were like mortar between the rough slabwork of the men.

Murdo stood there thoughtfully, his pea-head with its great flapping ears tilted forward on the scrawny stem of his neck. He, too, felt ill at ease dressed in his old blue suit, with the collar of his oversize shirt hanging round his neck like a halter. One of his enormous hands, knotty and cut, came up mindlessly and attempted to arrange some comfort in the collar. Behind the watery film of his eyes, the image of his woman, Margaret, persisted. He blinked and there out before him was the shape of his daughter, Flora, white and all white but for the blackness of her hair. And beside her, the thick frame of Hughie Morrison the man that, before God, she was taking to herself.

It was August 4th. And the image of Flora confused itself with that of her mother. For it was twenty-six years to the day that he, Murdo Munro, had stood there in that very kirk and taken young Margaret for his wife. How could this be? Was it really this same woman who now stood beside him? Young Margaret from the Borders. Pretty, young Margaret with her laughing eyes and her laughing ways.

Murdo frowned.

With her white skin and small hands and her rounded, hidden body whose image he had tried to chase from his mind with the drink when, for those long months, he had feared he would never win her. Month on month, she had been polite to him and no more; and he had despaired and longed all the more for her – for her body and perhaps her soul too. But gradually he had grown accustomed to longing for her and had come to accept his failure. That was how it had always come to him. So that when they had met by chance, one wild, winter's day on the road high above the village and had taken shelter together from a squall, he had stood sullenly by her beneath the overhang of black rock and thought of little beyond how long the rain would last. And then, against the sound of the rain, her light laugh had surfaced from their silence and he had turned to see her smiling at him.

'Och, Murdo Munro, you and your black thoughts!' she had laughed and with an inexplicable surge of his old passion he had seized her and kissed her fiercely. Later, in the chill, dank silence of his house in the village, he had sat down at the table by the window with tears running down his bony cheeks and there had been no way of telling whether this sudden childlike collapse was from happiness, relief or desperate, dark-rooted misery. A month later they were engaged and by that day in the following August they were man and wife.

It was hard for Murdo to follow the linking that connected the smiling young girl of his youth with the woman who stood beside him. The tears that had bubbled up from his staring eyes that winter's afternoon had perhaps been some deep-rising warning that the kiss given so impetuously on the hill had set in motion the beginning of his gradual decline. Aye, and a decline it had been. The first weeks – months even – of the marriage had passed well enough, buoyant with the hope of better things. But the better things had never come. He had felt himself open and willing, pliable and forgiving; and for a while Margaret had smiled back at him. But, without drama, they had moved apart. There had been no furious quarrel, no open contention to mark the onset of their failing relationship; but slowly a silence, heavy and cold as sheet metal, had raised itself between them. Murdo, with nowhere to go but the hotel bar when he wanted to get away from Margaret, had slipped into the age-old habit of drink, not finding escape in the alcoholic haze but sitting leaden-eyed before the pints of heavy and the oily drams with his mind closeted in his growing despair. To begin with, it had been bad but then once he had finally given up any hope of finding happiness with this woman, Murdo discovered that in some way he was strangely relieved to have returned to his old state of melancholy.

And what had Margaret felt, what had this woman really wanted of him? Murdo had no idea. But like many a strong-willed woman, she had turned all this to her advantage. She had taken her life out into the village and made herself into an irreplaceable part of the local life, befriending some, ingratiating herself with others and spiting the few who stood against her – and all the while speaking lovingly of her man. Even back in their home with its two ground-floor rooms and its upstairs bedrooms, she rarely bothered to curse and bite at Murdo but effectively crushed the last semblance of warmth between them by casually ignoring him. So long as he brought her the weekly money, she accepted his presence.

And then, in the second year of their marriage, she had got from Murdo the very thing which was to become the symbol of division between them. Late one evening in March, Margaret, full-grown with child, had sent Murdo out for the midwife. As he crunched and slithered his way along the street, he had been full of the hope that the coming bairn was going to set right the sadness of his marriage. Returning with the midwife, he had sat down by the fire and listened to the noises and silences in the room above. The hours had drifted by but finally, deep in the frozen stillness of the night, he had been roused from his dozing by a thin, rough-edged cry. A while later, the midwife had come down and told him that he could go up. Shyly he had crept into the bedroom to find Margaret lying with a small, wrinkled face clutched to her breast. And if the look on Margaret's face had been one of maternal joy, there might still have been the glimmer of redemption for Murdo and her. But her look was one of triumph and it told Murdo that the bairn was not to be theirs but hers alone.

From that day he and Margaret had scarcely spoken a word to each other on anything but practical matters. All Margaret's affection and love poured forth on to her daughter, Flora. Watching her smiling and kissing the

13

bairn, Murdo thought of what she and he might have shared and what they together might have been to Flora. The bairn was coddled with love and kept with jealous care from any possible closeness with its father. When Murdo was out at his work in the forests, the neighbours were brought in to coo around the unsuspecting infant; and on Sundays, when Murdo was about the house, Margaret would parade her little Flora up and down the village street. Margaret always spoke of the bairn as hers: Murdo and Flora were never mentioned in the same breath.

As the years passed Murdo settled himself into his role of spectator. And he drank. Never quite into the cage of alcoholism but into its ante-room that was peopled by so many of the islanders.

Flora grew up into a pretty, self-possessed girl with her mother's good looks and none of her father's black temperament. In fact, in his bouts of drinking, Murdo sometimes wondered if he had really fathered this bairn so little did she appear to be like him. She became one of the leaders of the village children, dominated the local school and, egged on by her mother, began to give herself airs as she grew into a young woman. But it was as if Margaret had given over to her daughter not only her life but also her physical well-being for as Flora blossomed so Margaret plunged steeply into a decline. Her body became fat and unmanageable in her clothes; then her face followed suit, leaving those wild, bright eyes pig-like and mean in the cushions of her cheeks; and her hair thinned and fell lank and lifeless.

All this Murdo Munro had watched with neither concern nor sorrow. So deeply had his former love for Margaret been buried by her coldness that it all passed before him chilled into unreality. As for Flora – it was difficult to say what kind of relationship he had, or might have had, with her. Her mother had taught her not hate but scorn towards

14

her father: something which drove Murdo still deeper into his drinking. For all the while, he suffered from a silent, stifled love for his daughter. He loved her in that generous but self-destructive way of unrelieved secrecy which bore a strange resemblance to his earlier longing for Margaret. The only outlet for his passion was to work long hours in the knowledge that the money gained would give the bairn the material things she needed. But he longed to be able to do more than this; and when Margaret used his sweated money to buy Flora a present and the girl threw her arms round her mother's neck in pleasure and happiness, Murdo would watch from across the room, warmly, but with his soul transfixed by what he was denied.

'O God, who in Thy great mercy . . .'

Murdo bowed his head as the prayer began. He had been brought up in the tradition of the kirk and was by nature a religious man though with little understanding of the minister's words or any of the tenets of the kirk. As always, the unworldly rhythm of the service held his inner being fascinated, poised on the brink of happiness. There was some strange feeling, a dim awareness of it offering everything that he had been refused by the world, a feeling of warmth and awe and longing.

He glanced up and the minister's eyes were fixed on him. As he looked down again he took in the shape of his daughter, white as a gull's neck, beside the heavy build of her man. She, the sole balance to his life, was going. And with the suddenness of some delayed understanding it came to him that this day, this service was the end of his life.

August 4th! On this day, twenty-six years ago, he had stood before the Revd Alexander Donaldson and had felt that his life was beginning. Now he stood there again to witness the departure of his daughter into her new world. With Flora gone, what position would he hold in his own house? Slowly the full dimensions of the future drew up their grim shapes before him. Years of pointless silence and loneliness under the same roof as Margaret? And when retirement came and there was no longer the daily escape into work, what then? The dull flutterings of panic turned in Murdo's stomach.

Out on the slopes of Beinn an Eòin, far above the head of the loch, the breeze shimmered and puffed and the land was stirred.

Murdo looked at Hughie Morrison. He was a good lad, right enough, strong and dependable, with a steady job over on the estate at Dorusduan. He would provide for Flora well enough, there was no worry in that. And before the bairns came, Flora would be able to continue her work at the shop. No, they'd not want for anything. The lassie would be all right.

He thought of the other villagers behind him in the kirk. He knew them all well enough but now they were nothing to him as his mind was caught up in the flowerings of new hope. Only old Donnie MacGillivray, a seventy-five-year-old bachelor, who was his drinking companion, came before his eyes as a reality. Well, there was always something to leave behind.

The minister's supplications and the congregation's growing responses drifted away into the middle distance. Murdo bent forward and leaned on the back of the pew in front. He stared down at the hard wooden bench.

Again the breeze gave itself out in an increase of strength. And once again Murdo recalled the minister's words that had lived in a corner of his mind since a Sunday service some weeks before:

'If your right eye causes you to sin, pluck it out and throw it away; it is better that you lose one of your members than that your whole body be thrown into hell. And if your right hand causes you to sin, cut it off and throw it

16

away; it is better that you lose one of your members than that your whole body go into hell.' God have mercy on me a sinner!

The family, the old sacred unit of the glens, was at risk. With Flora gone, the body was reduced to the man and his woman who must, in the inevitable drawing-in and cramping of old age, carry each other into hell. That was the dark way in which things appeared to Murdo Munro this August afternoon at his daughter's wedding.

And with the self-reproaching glory of the melancholic, he knew for sure that he alone was the offending member that was to be severed from the body. Margaret had made a life for herself (whether it was good or bad was beyond his understanding) and it was he who was the hindrance. This he realized and nothing else, no practical consider-ations, mattered.

His mouth and chin twisted violently to the left and his head stretched forward in a series of ludicrous contrac-tions, a nervous twitch that turned his already scraggy and disjointed features into a mad tangle – something which the bairns in the village loved to imitate. He felt his woman staring at him.

The twitch continued again and again, ever more strongly. Out on the crags of Beinn an Eòin a ragged hoodie was catapulted skywards by a new thrust of wind.

There was a sudden pause in the service as Hughie Morrison fumbled for the ring. In the silence Murdo spoke softly but clearly:

'Aye,' he said. 'Aye . . . and so it is.'

And the breeze blew no more.

'Murdo!' Margaret hissed at him. 'Murdo!'

He straightened up slowly, entranced, and looked round into her face. Beneath her squat blue hat, the eyes, peeled of affection, threatened him. The mouth was drawn into a tight ring of determination in the lardy cheeks.

17

He sighed deeply and spoke:

'I must away out a wee while.'

'Murdo, you can't go, not now. For heaven's sake, man!'

'What? I must away out. I'll no be long.'

'Murdo Munro, I tell you wait. Are you wanting to shame us all?'

Murdo paused and lowered his glazy eyes before the threat of his woman. Then gently but firmly:

'I know well enough what you're saying, woman; but you've to let me be. I've to be away out for a moment.' And as his woman prepared to remonstrate, Murdo Munro moved resolutely past her bulk and out into the aisle.

He caught a glimpse of Flora turning; he caught other glimpses of Mairi Patterson and Jenny Melville frowning beneath their neat bonnets; he heard vague murmurs and felt glances from along the pews on both sides. But, with his ambling clumsy gait, he passed down the aisle, carving his way through the conventions of the villagers. His steps, crisp and steel, sounded out the measures of his new resolution. The colours of the wedding clothes flowed bubbling by his sides and then were gone and he issued forth between the dark, oaken doors of the kirk.

The moment before he left the kirk, he was one of the village congregation and the half-view of the road outside was almost beyond his reach. His resolution wavered. And then with a pace more he was out and part of the land and the circling ocean, with the blue veil and the combings of the high cirrus standing far above; and the people of Acheninver, the witnesses of his years of defeat, were, quite suddenly, behind him and were unreal figures of the past.

Murdo blinked and rubbed his chin with the back of his horny hand. A hedgehog lay curled on the verge. A beech tree, still and immensely strong, was suddenly ruffled for a moment by a straggler from the afternoon breezes.

Murdo walked up the small slope of the road and turned into the main street. Apart from the scatter of houses lying in the outer neighbourhood, this one street constituted the village of Acheninver. A hundred yards of roadway with two columns of low buildings huddling close to the tarmac for security. The houses themselves were mainly single-storeyed with a window or two in the roof; though every now and again there was a larger building with a full second storey. Since there was such little difference in the construction of the houses, the distinguishing features lay in the details of their exterior finish. Many were grey and harsh in their clothing of stone; some were thinly white-washed; while a few others – holiday houses owned by visitors from the south – were smartly painted with the woodwork picked out in bright colours. The houses were pleasant enough but there was a complex air of con-nivance, of incest in the way in which they crowded together while in all directions the hills and water and doming sky expanded without limit.

Murdo passed the Acheninver Hotel which stood like a guard post at the entrance to the village street. The rough forecourt, the crates of empty bottles, the plain green door to the bar – these familiar details touched open the springs of his memory for it was here that he had sought refuge from his marriage all those long years. He pursed his lips bitterly and turned away, leaving behind him a tangled wake of visions.

As he reached the first houses, he stopped in the middle of the road and stared ahead of him. Virtually everyone was in the kirk and the village stood, an empty shell, sullen and unfeeling, watching to see how this man would turn. Slated roofs shored up the unmeasured weight of the sky; a high attic window drank up the light of the sun in a trapped explosion; a low doorway gaped humid and dank in the shadow of its opponent across the street; a thick cluster of elder, rank and miserable, sprouted in the narrow space between two buildings. Beneath the surface of peace slid the well-camouflaged but voracious image of finality.

How was he to leave all this? Each stone, every corner, every detail awoke some memory in his turbid mind. The memories were mostly bad, carrying incidents of sadness and pain from over the years. Even the few good moments, way back in the first months he had known Margaret, even those sparse memories of happiness were cast down by what had become of them. Aye, Acheninver had seen him pass through black years. And yet this was what he knew, this was what constituted his life. Bad as it had been, how could he, a man in his fifties, hack through all that had gone before and cast off into an unforeseeable future? People just did not do that. A man grew up, got himself a job, a house, a woman, bairns – and whether he liked it or not they would be his till he died. Was it not always like that?

Murdo shuffled his feet on the rough tarmac and, for a moment, his heart sagged, tugged downwards by fear. He must stop his madness and go back to the kirk. Go back to what was real – his woman, his home, his responsibilities and his future. He had survived twenty-six years of it. He had seen other men living out their lives in similar circumstances, bending themselves before the demands of convention and waiting passively for the release of death. They found their small compensations and amusements, somehow . . . so why should he, Murdo Munro, think himself the man to make a change in all that?

He looked along the street towards his house which stood slightly back from the roadway at the far end of the village. His face puckered and twitched and his hands, big as paddles, hung limply at his sides. He stayed like this for a while, quite still, only his eyes moving, wandering here and there ceaselessly in search of a resolution.

Then, far above, a herring gull split open the silence in a relentless series of calls, violent and piercing. Murdo's head went back and he gazed at the circling bird, a white cross halfway down in the ocean depths of the sky. Now it swung and planed in silence, its head pricking round sporadically to look down at the man who appeared as a small growth rooted in the gorge of the village street.

Then again, as if filled by something outside itself, the bird's cry burst out, bugling and wailing without pause until the whole sky was covered by its webbing echoes, until it seemed as if everything in sight must give way and wait in deference to the creature's power. On and on it cried, the smooth rhythm of its flight detached, undisturbed, the sunlight firing its white breast. Once again it fell into a brief silence, and then, with two final cries, it turned and headed away northwards and out of sight behind the skyline.

The new stillness, bounded by the warmth of the sun and the smell of the land, sweet and sharp, cradled Murdo's mind, lulled it, brought it a peace and clarity hitherto unknown to him. For a few brief seconds everything beyond his own immediate consciousness was distanced, a mere reflection of the rest of the world, something quite separate from his existence. His woman, his daughter, his work – all the material components of his married life – were no more than small details of his twenty-six years of sadness. They were no longer unbending obligations but merely hindrances to the indestructible hopes of joy that he could not help but carry within, even perhaps to the edge of the grave. Not hopes of success, wealth or even happiness – mere surface features – but hopes of finding resolution, unspoken joy, peace in the very centre of his warring soul. All this came to Murdo in the form of an instinct, seemingly meaningless, yet vital nonetheless.

And with the single-mindedness of an animal following an instinct, he broke out of his trance and stepped forward along the street.

He marched between the houses conscious of their blind-eyed scrutiny. He walked on, crunching the glassy silence with his footsteps, his face twitching and contorting from time to time as his mind wrestled with his plans. Occasionally his pace slowed for a moment. He moved as if lost.

'Who'll that be?'

A shrill voice darted forth unowned from a house whose front door stood ajar. Murdo started.

'It'll be yon man, I tell you: aye, it's time enough and I know the sound of his steps. Well, be off with you! That's no way to be walking by the now!' Old Annie McPherson, a bedridden widow, simple as a child these eight years past, called out in her garbled fashion. Murdo was about to answer her, calm her with a few words, but he thought better of it and hurried on to his house.

It stood back from the main line of houses on the eastern side of the street. A short path of cinders led from the roadway to the small squat building with its grey door and shining windows. Margaret had grown some flowers in window-boxes and the whole exterior, recently white-washed, looked cheerful and friendly. The two downstairs windows were framed with bright red curtains while up in the roof the yellow and blue curtains of the front bedroom stood out sharply against the slates. Murdo pushed open the front door and went in.

The cheerful aspect of the house was the final humiliation for him. It was the cruelness of the public pretence which aggrieved him. Flowers and bright colours and warmth and tidiness were a lie, a day-to-day deceit when all that filled his soul was darkness. For twenty-six years he had borne this in unthinking silence, accepting that the arrangement of the house was the woman's domain; yet struggling to assuage the rankling sore that he suffered from this unvoiced taunt. Flora had deflected him from such black thoughts for he had wanted the bairn to grow up amidst warmth and light in the hope that such things would cover the shadows that lay between her parents. But now, with her gone, a frantic urge for the truth to be shown fired up in Murdo's mind. This day, coming at the end of such a long period of submission, brought to Murdo a fierce determination. The wind had blown deep into his being.

Murdo stood in the little sitting-room. The shiny, cherry-red armchairs faced emptily into the grate. The collection of china dolls and animals on the mantelpiece were crowned by a print in which a beribboned cat gazed stupidly out into the room. A vase of plastic flowers stood on the window sill. The walls were a mass of patterned flowers and fruit. The horde of blunt colours jangled before his eyes, baffling and teasing him. A dull wave of fury broke across his soul and he slumped into a chair, covering his face with his hands.

Behind his rough palms, the view he saw every day from up in the forest unfolded itself. For the vast expanses of the island hills to the south of Acheninver always filled him with a strange nostalgia. And now his covered eyes followed the long shapes, the heathers dark and swelling, the open plateaux quickened with hidden life, the land rising in rounds and hummocks of grass marked with purple-black patches of rock and run with secret cuts, blue and coal, where small burns carried themselves downwards from the seclusion of the high hills. The land surged and fell and surged away again into the distance; and then, lastly, was drawn up in massive leaps. Its gentle momentum had gathered and grown until it was no longer to be contained and, through the sharp wind which was forever curling and thrusting across that first spiny ridge, it rose up beneath the sun. As if nothing could stop its steepening ascent past crags and brief summits, it finally sprang up to meet the burning hard light. At last, high above the glens and crofts, it shed its downy coat of grasses and exploded with the sunlight in the rocky crown that was known as A' Mhaighdean, the Maiden.

Murdo saw this and his heart tightened.

Deep in the cavern of his hands, he smelt too the airs, now thick with peat and sweet mosses, now cold and hard with wet rock, now wafery and sharp with blueness and light. He felt the brushing of brackens at his thighs; the cushioning spring of warm grasses in a forest clearing; heard the long willowing spill of the curlew plaiting with the heron's rasp against the clarity of the dampened coast in the half-light . . . All this was quite remote from his life in the village; he thought of it solely in connection with his work, often solitary, far out in the forest. But over the years of his marriage, it had come to be what was real.

He trembled. His rough nails dug into his forehead. His eyes and mouth pinched tight. His large ungainly feet stuck out before him, as solid and heavy as if they were no part of the turmoil in his brain. Rhythmically, he ground his palms against his eyeballs, trying to suppress the tension in his ragged head. The dull contours of a hymn carried their way to him from the kirk and threw out the last semblance of control from his thoughts. He felt himself being torn apart, savaged by all the strands of hope and despair, fear and courage. The complexity of the situation had temporarily crushed the reason and clarity in him, had driven him outwards from his narrow existence until, with a last blow, he was cast over into the areas of sheer instinct.

With a violent gesture, he tore his hands from his eyes. His gaping vision was veiled by sliding and diving shapes and colours, stars, vipers and amoebic growths. From their midst, the cat gazed at him.

'Aye, by Christ!' The words stamped out sharply on the silence.

Now he got up quickly and walked out of the room. Sounds were heard upstairs and a moment later he clattered down again in his working clothes. A heavy blue sweater, stained denim trousers and tackety boots. He looked in at the sitting-room again, his rheumy eyes fixed and determined.

In the kitchen he packed his piece-bag with food, took the money that he found in a tin behind the sugar-bowl and went out of the back door. He returned carrying a can of petrol. He poured the petrol over the chairs and carpet in the sitting-room and used the last drops to make a trail of it as a fuse. From out in the hall he looked bitterly into the sitting-room once more, struck a match and lit the fuse. With a mild explosion, the trail of petrol ignited and flames scuttered hastily towards the sitting-room. Murdo seized his old thornproof coat and hat off the hook and walked out of the house closing the back door behind him. He bowed his head for a moment and then stepped out into the wilderness of grasses, nettles and tall foxgloves which separated the building from the open land. He hated the nettles with their sour smell of decay and trod them down with a vigour in his eagerness to get clear of the village. There was that nervous excitement in him, that kicking heart and clutched throat that is part of the fear of being caught in an irresponsible action.

He sprang clear of the nettles, splashed his way across a foul-smelling ditch and came out at the foot of the brae which sheltered the village from the east. Without a pause he set off upwards, cutting diagonally across it towards the north-east. Already he was panting from the fast pace but he never slowed, only raising his head from time to time to gauge the distance to a fistful of pines that stood up on the ridge above him.

Faster and faster he climbed, his gangly, crab-like movements strengthened by his fear of being seen. The pines spiked into the soft sky above him as he reached the final steep slope to the ridge. Safety lay within his call.

At that moment, a child's cry rang out behind him, sharp and thin in the still, warm airs. He kicked and clutched at the springing tussocks, heaved and pulled himself over the lip of the rise and into the shadow of the trees. Wide-eyed and gasping, dry-mouthed and dizzy he collapsed on to the bed of pine needles. Had he been seen? He rolled over on to his stomach and crawled back to peer over the ridge.

There below him the village of Acheninver stood in its neat lines. From his house smoke flowered and curled like a great black vine. A young boy was running back down the street in the direction of the kirk, shouting the news of the fire. A large black mongrel pranced and bounded around him, caught up in the sudden excitement. Over at the kirk, Flora's white figure stood with her man at the doorway among a group of friends.

Murdo buried his face in the earth. What, in God's name, had he gone and done?

Up the road from the kirk to the village street ran a little chain of people.

The smoke thickened. For a moment it was flattened across the house by a breath of wind and the building was masked. As the drifting smoke cleared, Murdo saw the first fruit of the vine, a yellow-red burnished tendril, leap and coil upwards. It sank down as if lacking in strength but immediately snaked out again accompanied by another. The fire was under way.

Murdo Munro rolled away from the scene and lay on his back gazing solemnly up at the hatching of pine and sky. A thin, hopeless smile broke out on his face and he closed his eyes for a brief moment to look out on to a countryside without horizons.

CHAPTER TWO

The bannock-like island of Eilean na Rainich was, in fact,
the top of a long, hidden arm of Am Bodha Ruadh, a
sunken reef lying five hundred yards to the west which the
fishermen skirted widely in all weathers. Its small area,
once cultivated, was now a mass of brackens growing in
places to the height of a man's chest. Scarcely any clear
ground was visible except at the eastern end where an
outcrop of gnarled rock thrust up out of a ring of grass. Its
shoreline was a continuous strip of blackened stone and
weed. This small protrusion of land and the coast of the
main island were joined underwater by a further extension
of the reef's arm so that the channel between the two,
some hundred yards at high tide, was a mere fifteen feet
deep. It was well over a hundred years since anyone had
bothered to try and work the little island's few acres of
usable ground.

At the moment that Murdo was leaving the small clutch
of pine trees and walking northwards away from Acheninver, Eilean na Rainich, Am Bodha Ruadh and the handful
of other skerries and grass-topped rocks that lay scattered
along that stretch of the island's northern coast were all
lying flat and dilated by the heat of the long summer's day.
Out here, there was enough of a breeze to crinkle large
tracts of the ocean wastes so that the surface of the sea was
made up of odd streaks, rivers and counter-running patterns inside which there lay breathing long patches of
oily-skinned water trapped in the lee of the land. Against
the coast itself the sea endlessly grew and died across the
layers of rock and tangle, setting up changing rhythms of
sound and movement. In among the rocks, there echoed

the minute slappings and suckings of water: but this ceaseless noise was often dominated by moments of greater action as the hidden swell rose over a broad-shouldered rock in fringes of foam and then fell back on itself. As the water fell, the rock was momentarily encased in a mould of perfect uniformity, suggesting softness beneath the sheen – and then, once more, the illusion passed and the rock, rough and barnacled, stood proud of the sea. But nothing was ever quite complete for each backwash sent its currents and eddies out to cross with those of nearby rocks. Though the confusion was immeasurable, behind it there seemed an underlying plan, for the sea offshore that delivered the swell was ordered and calm.

A short way out, some rafts of tangle floated half-submerged; a water-logged fishbox knocked against a rock; some terns circled with their sprung, limping flight. Further off, a small colony of skarts fished insatiably, swimming along head down and then leaping out to disappear sleekly into the depths. Far out beyond, the sea expanded to unseen dimensions, overrunning everything except in the distance to the north where occasional islands pressed their high, serrate forms upwards into the haze.

And over the sounds of the idly flapping sea, over the myriad salted smells of the shore, hung the all-engulfing, motionless heat.

There was still an hour or so to go before sunset when Murdo finally appeared on the skyline. Two hours before, with the shouts and clamours from the village street battering about in his head, he had slipped away down the far side of the hill leaving the group of pines high above him like a mountain frontier post. Coming down off the soft, shiny grasses he had set off along a sheep track which led northwards across the undulating hills. Having set fire to his own house, he had turned unthinkingly towards the forest, the one place he knew which would afford him cover while he made his plans. For the moment at least, he knew where he was going.

He walked hurriedly, the piece-bag and thornproof bouncing on his hip, his body thrown forwards and his arms swinging widely as if to propel himself faster. He passed over several low hills and then, having climbed up the back of a small escarpment, he came out above the edge of the forest. Below him, the ranks of pine and larch stretched away into the distance, bending over the shoulders of the land, filling each fold, flooding in their regular bands onwards to a far hillside where their mass was checked in a rigidly straight line. Through a dip in the skyline, the rim of the sea showed itself, a chalice of blue. At the near side of the forest could be seen the immense weight of purple darkness which hung suspended from the lower branches of the trees.

Murdo scrambled down the rocks, eager for the safety of the forest. He followed the high, stranded fence north-wards for a short way until he came to a barred gate. Here he let himself in and vanished into the trees.

The gate closed with a rich, heavy sound. He walked quickly down the ride for several minutes until it turned slightly, leaving him hidden from outside. Only then did he stop. Encircled by the trees of his everyday work, Murdo felt himself at home. He stood there with his hands on his hips, looking round about him, his confidence slowly gathering. His consciousness was overwhelmed by the hammering of pulses and the whistling of his breath. But gradually his body calmed and, immeasurably there gathered about him the warm and resinous cloakings of the summer afternoon's silence. And as he waited so, like rising bubbles, the sounds that made up the silence came forward. Nearby, a yellowhammer called; deeper in the forest a bullfinch piped weakly. The trickling of a burn, nowhere visible, was somewhere close at hand. A large bee droned by. From time to time a faint breeze rooted half-heartedly among the tree-tops. Murdo heard it all, blinked, slowly scratched his ear and then sniffed violently.

Murdo Munro's house in Acheninver had been council property. As the safety of the forest began to give him strength and support so too did the full realization of what he had done come to him. A council house purposely burnt down by its tenant was something which the authorities would most likely hand over directly to the police. He began to wonder what he should do.

It was remarkable that Murdo should have got so far without seriously considering what he was going to do. But he had acted in a dull frenzy of pain and misery in which there had been no place for everyday logic. And, indeed, it was this very impulsiveness, this angry blindness that had given him his freedom: for, in a calmer state of mind, he would have seen the irredeemable rashness of such a thing. And there was little place for rashness in a community such as that of Acheninver. Yet in the dull channels of Murdo's thoughts there was still no regret. Shame and floating fear filled him. Fear of being pursued, fear of being lost, adrift, without food or shelter, aye . . . but no regrets. Anything was preferable to the pointless resignation of his life with his woman. But the courage was still lacking. His tangled face, blotchy red around the water-blue eyes, hung limp.

For the moment he must find a place to lie hidden for a day or two. In spite of his first instincts, he decided that the forest was not safe. It would probably be one of the first places they would look. He needed to get off the island . . .

He scratched vigorously at the scabby edge of his ear. For a minute or two he wandered around, hands in his pockets, kicking at an old tree stump. Then suddenly he stopped, smiled grimly, shrugged and set off down the ride again.

Now he walked purposefully. His old boots sprang energetically on the turf, his arms swung out, the thin greasy hair was flattened back in one movement of a knotty hand; his eyes, set in determination, looked up at the sun. Murdo Munro felt himself, if nothing else, free.

Using the rides, he gradually made his way towards the northern edge of the forest. He sweated heavily in the close air of the plantation and was surrounded by clouds of midges and clegs which rose from the undergrowth. He was accustomed to them but cursed angrily as if as a vent for the pressure within him. At one moment he paused on a long slope and looking back southwards over the forest, he saw the glistening crest of A' Mhaighdean rising in the distance behind its foothills. He turned away quickly, irritated or shamed or saddened by his memories. Up ahead of him, a fang of blue bit deep into the dark green wall of the trees.

At the top of the slope he came to the end of the forest. Letting himself out through a gate, he felt a light breeze lick at the sweat of his forehead. He walked out over the heathers and found himself on the ridge above Eilean na Rainich. The sea and the sky, double blue, formed an effortless, airy dome about his being. After the warmth and tightness of the forest, he felt lightheaded with the expansive, polished peace of the sea beneath him. He laughed out loud and ran down the slope, cutting eastwards towards a deep fold in the shoreland where a mass of small birch trees grew. As he went, he cast nervous, exploratory glances back along the coast.

When he reached the edge of the fold where the birch trees grew, Murdo came slowly and cautiously over the skyline. Down below him ran a burn which opened out into a wide pool. At the seaward end of the pool, the water poured out through a channel in the soft rock. This pool was known as the Poll nam Morbh and was where, long ago, the men used to come with their fish-spears to take the salmon and sea-trout. Now it lay on the western edge of the Dorusduan Estate and was fished mainly by poachers. A cart track came across the hills from the east and down to the edge of the pool where a small boat lay moored to a stake.

Murdo came down through the trees, slithering and sliding on the banks of moss and mud and dead leaves. He crossed the burn above the pool and made his way round to the boat. He sauntered up and down for a minute or two, looking the boat over and eyeing the entrance to the channel. Finally, he glanced up the track and, throwing his coat and bag into the boat, untied the rope and climbed in.

He rowed out into the middle of the pool and then turned towards the narrow channel. Some five foot across and with steep, rocky sides, it now looked daunting. He gave one sharp pull on the oars, glanced over his shoulder and straightened the boat and then let the current take him. He sat there, twisted on the bench seat, watching the channel as the boat crept ever nearer. Slowly, but so slowly, the bows were sucked towards the sluicing of the plug-dark waters. And then, at the last moment, there was the sudden silent acceleration and they were into the channel and Murdo was turning from side to side in his efforts to keep the boat off the rocky walls. He pushed too hard at one side, barked his knuckles and as the boat ground into the opposite wall, he was thrown from the seat. As he clambered to his feet, the boat passed from the mouth of the burn into the buoyant flashings of the sea. The boat soon lost its momentum and Murdo, peering over the gunwale, saw through the water's greenness, rock and sand and sleeping weed.

He scanned the coast for anyone who might have seen

him. Then, taking the oars, he began to row back towards Eilean na Rainich. He had little experience with boats and rowed badly, catching crabs and failing to hold a straight course. The water lapped and clucked at the bows as they rode over the smooth surface. The sun shone bright as ever, the breeze was light and Murdo felt himself free of the island. A gull hung inquisitively over the wake. Minutes later, Murdo brought the boat in on the seaward side of the little island. Wedging it between two boulders, he secured it as best he could and waded through the knee-deep water to the shore.

The sun was beginning to fall.

He crossed the belt of blackened stones and entered the brackens, heading towards the mound of rock. When he bent his head to see where he was going, he all but disappeared from sight. At the foot of the rock, he found a small opening, a kind of half-cave. Here he threw down his coat and bag, and, climbing up to a thick growth of heathers above the cave, began to collect himself a makeshift bed. Heaving and ripping, he dislodged a number of large roots which he tossed down to the opening below. He straightened up, sniffed, blew his nose between thumb and forefinger, wiped his hand on his trouser leg and sprang down from the rock.

He pushed the mass of heathers into the opening, tried it with his hand and then sat down. He opened his piece-bag and began to eat. His jaw worked massively. As he ate, he kept passing his hand over his face. When he had finished, he scratched his ear, belched and stared out into the sunset.

A thin wind had got up with the approach of evening. The sea, light-blue beneath a shivering skin of quicksilver, lay in clearly defined strips. Murdo gazed up and saw, high above, the transparent deepings of the sky: lower down, nearer the long ribbings of cloud which streaked the horizon, it had a whitened, floury look. Between the clouds and the horizon itself, it seemed as if that far edge of the world were covered by an immense sandstorm; for the whole area, including the islands further round to the north, was thick with a dusty light. The track which the sun burned across the sea wavered fluidly; while the sun itself, unbearably bright only minutes before, was now yellowing with age.

Slowly the horizon was being drawn into the forge of the falling sun. The pillar of flame on the sea was breaking up. Across the whole of the western skyline there were signs of collapse as everything was enveloped by the roaring haze. And then, suddenly, as if finally ceding to the pressures of the coming night, the sun cooled to a dull orange, took on a soft redness and, touching the horizon, speedily vanished from sight. At once the sky loosened and thinned, the layers of colour separating and the surface of the sea becoming a scaly sheet of black and silver under the spreading cover of the night.

And so it was that on the evening of his daughter's wedding day, Murdo Munro sat alone on a small island and watched the sun go down across the open plains of the Atlantic. He sat huddled on his meagre bed of heathers for a while longer and then, wrapping his thornproof tight about him, he turned his back on the sea and lay down to sleep.

He lay there with his arms about his head, his eyes closed, waiting for sleep to come. Somewhere along the coast a flock of oystercatchers trilled. The sea slapped on the nearby rocks. Far, far away a boat's diesel engine tapped on the silence. Murdo shifted slightly. The sketchings of the night wind coiled in off the sea.

Time passed. And with its passing came the complete night and the ascending power of the moon's milk-rich light.

Murdo lay as before but now with eyes staring into the black shadows thrown by his body on the rock. With systematic harshness, his mind was passing from one problem to the next. Looking deep into the void before him, he waited motionless with a childlike belief that an answer would eventually present itself . . .

There were people back on the island who would take him in, for sure; but it would only be a matter of time before he was seen. So whatever happened, he needed to get away. But how? He would be recognized on the ferries; and the fishermen he knew all worked out of the main port . . . If only he could get to the mainland! This was the major problem that beset him. Once on the mainland he would go to Bessie: that he had already decided. He had a boat, right enough; but three miles in a rowing boat across such an exposed stretch of water . . . Murdo closed his eyes tightly. Perhaps he should go back, try and cross the island and find somebody in the south to take him off . . . And so the man's tremulous mind set off once again on tracks of chaos and despair. From dead-end after dead-end he retraced his steps and set off in search of new, untried lines of thought. And somewhere far out in those featureless and lonely plains of his mind, his waking thoughts moved imperceptibly into those of dreams.

The moon shone brilliantly from a clear sky. A cool wind wove in among itself. Together they created faint but voluptuous patterns along the coast, stroking at the waters before turning across the foreshore and running up over the grasses to enter the edge of the sleeping forest, where they minutely but endlessly split the blackness of the trees. Occasionally, odd, untraceable splashings told of the presence of sea-birds; otherwise the only sound apart from the wind was the sporadic barking of a dog behind the hills towards Dorusduan.

Murdo jerked in his sleep. He lay in a curled position,

his knees drawn up to his chest to retain his warmth. Twice more he started, groaned bitterly from the depths of his sleep and then was awake, eyes wide-open beneath the rock. He sat up brusquely, with no recollection of where he was. He was chilled to the bone. The sudden awakening after the turmoil of his dreams left him with a pumping heart. Dreams of guilt and shame; dreams in which Flora and the minister had been present.

He jumped to his feet, cupped his hands and blew into them and rubbed himself all over as much in an attempt to ward off the rising panic as to warm himself.

He must get away. He had to move. Sleep had now completely left him. The coming day would find him trapped. Everybody would be on the look-out for him. He looked out to sea. With the water as calm as it was and under the light of the moon, the crossing would be much the same as it would be in daylight. But the night-time sea . . . a glittering tautness suspended over unmeasured chasms of silence. Yet he must, he must. For the waiting was worse.

Impelled by this fit of panic, he seized his things and picked his way down through the brackens to the shape of the boat. Twice he stumbled in the dark ferns and fell. Twice he swore softly. His legs trembled. For a moment he wished he were dead: past fear and decisions.

He untied the boat, which had risen high between the rocks with the flooding tide, climbed aboard and carefully poled out into the waiting sea. When he felt a good depth of water beneath him, he sat down and looked around. Already the shore seemed to have lost its dimensions, a black smudge between water and land. Westwards, the constant movement of the sea around Am Bodha Ruadh was hard to distance. Eastwards, beneath the moon, the long line of the coast ended in a beaklike promontory hooked fast into the water. Behind him, to the north-east, the arm of the mainland where he was planning to go was a delicately cut mass against the chill flesh of the sky.

Murdo stared along the promontory. He would best keep to the coast as far as the point and then strike out north across the open sea. He took the boat out into slightly deeper water and turned eastwards. The boat had a deceptive feeling of strength and security as it sliced through the silver-dark water. Murdo took his time, glancing over his shoulder and trying to gauge the distance to the point. As he moved down the coast, the land revealed itself as in a dream – the ashen gloss of the moonlit grasses, the pitch of the forest shadows, and later, the white slab of the Dorusduan Home Farm, deathly cold against the trees. Murdo watched all this in a state of disbelief. The water pattered and slapped; the wind fluttered over his face and hands. He was passing through an abandoned world. He swallowed slowly and bent his back into the oars. He should soon be at the point.

And as the tip of the promontory came into sight over his left shoulder, Murdo started to turn the boat out to sea. The first pull on the oars brought it round considerably; but as he raised them for the next stroke he noticed that the stern was swinging back again. Puzzled, he pulled harder but this time the boat scarcely changed its line at all. Indeed it seemed almost to move in the opposite direction. Murdo stopped rowing, the oars suspended over the water like stark wings. It was not easy to judge in the moonlight but he had the feeling that the boat was drifting in towards the promontory, its bows being gradually swung round in that direction. He turned the boat violently away from the land and gave three fierce pulls on the oars. Pausing, he watched the water. The whorls and eddies left by the oars were close together, still almost beside the boat. It was as if the boat were stationary.

Turning round on the seat, Murdo suddenly saw the

moonlight falling on waters cut and wrinkled by a powerful current. It was this that was carrying the boat in on the promontory which now lay only forty or fifty yards away.

'By Christ, it'll be the Rubh' a' Choin!'

He sprang to the oars, took the boat full round till it was running with the flow and then pulled strongly on the port side to bring it clear of the current. Seconds later, the boat lay wallowing in the dead water near the coast. Murdo's heart battered in his chest. He coughed and spat.

Though he had never actually seen it before, Murdo had heard the fishermen talk of the Rubh' a' Choin. It was a long, sharp promontory forming the north-eastern corner of the island where a heavy current swept in tight round the point and then drove on southwards along the coast. The fishing boats coming up against it from the south and wanting to turn the point had to work hard to pass through.

Murdo sat slumped over the oars. There was no chance of crossing the current which ran the Rubh 'a 'Choin, that he knew. He thought of letting the current take him past the point and down to where it weakened and then rowing back northwards on the other side of it. But where did the rocks lie on the far side of the point? Where in the silent turmoil of those waters that poured down in the shadow of the land, where was there a safe passage for the boat?

He paddled around in a desultory fashion. The moon shone down on the waters immovably. Murdo's face twisted and his neck and jaw were gripped by spasms as he tried to avoid facing the impossibility of the situation. If he could not pass through, then he must go back – but what then?

He rowed up beside the current tentatively, felt the bows being taken again and quickly backed off. Up and down he rowed, looking at the current from new angles and lines of approach, up and down he rowed in the

moonlight, sickness in his soul, his whole future seemingly blocked by this stream of water which unremittingly
coiled and bubbled its way past the Rubh' a' Choin.

And then, in sudden surrender to circumstance, he
turned the boat and began to row back along the coast
towards Eilean na Rainich. His back ached, his feet were
cold and wet. His gaze lay low over the sea, his eyes heavy
with tiredness and frustration. There was no further point
in it, he thought. He longed only for the deep oblivion of
sleep.

Arriving back at Eilean na Rainich, Murdo stood up to
try and guide the boat in. He poled gently with one oar
and with a blunt thud ran directly into a sunken rock. The
blow threw him off balance so that he lurched forward and
fell over the seat, knocking his shin and then catching his
elbow on the gunwale as he landed. He picked himself up
and stood rubbing the bruised bones.

Back at the cave, he sank on to the heathers, wrapped
himself as best he could in his coat and prepared to sit out
the night. For a while he continued to turn over all the old
possibilities. Then, sick to despair of these thoughts, he lay
down and drew his thornproof over his head. Perhaps
they had managed to put the fire out and the house had
not been too badly damaged. Perhaps he ought to go back
and try and patch things up . . .

Just as Murdo dropped off to sleep again, the eastern
skyline began to thrust up its first washes of grey and
white light. All over the great spread of the island, animals
began to shift and stir, preparing for the best hours of the
day, silent and cool, when they would go forth, the hun-
ters and the hunted. A small flock of goosanders rounded
the Rubh' a' Choin, and, turning west across the current,
flew fast and low over the water in the thin, pre-dawn
light. On the land, a few sheep were already at work
cropping the dewy grasses. Above them, the stubble of the

forest tree-tops was a honed outline on the buttery whiteness of the sky. Falling and rising in and out of sight against the light, a sparrowhawk ran the edge of the trees.

On Eilean na Rainich, Murdo Munro lay like a corpse.

CHAPTER THREE

Murdo's tackety boots and his woollen socks that lay on the rock beside him were fast drying in the heat of the mid-morning sun. He himself sat on the rock hunched forward, his elbows on his knees, staring down into a sea-pool. The pool had the completeness and purity of a small, hidden loch. Its surface, sheltered by the surrounding rocks and boulders, was still and untouched, lending the impression to the world beneath of having come into existence with that very day's dawn. Through the glossiness of the surface could be seen plum-like anemones, vine-growths of mussels, limpets, weed, minnows and small crabs. On the bottom of the pool was a bright array of different coloured rocks and pebbles in among which were little clusters of crushed and broken shell, already half sand. The water might have shattered if touched.

The silence and perspectiveless depth of the pool held Murdo lulled and entranced as he sat there caught up in his thoughts under the hot sun. Twice he blinked and twice his jaw jerked as he tried to keep his eyes focused. He rubbed at his shin and stared sightlessly into the pool.

He had slept on long after the sun's rising. Gradually the seashore had come alive with the screechings and squawkings of the terns and gulls; and, as if incited by this, the sheep too had set up some kind of irregular chorus that had echoed up and down the coast behind Eilean na Rainich. But Murdo, unwittingly adding to the tumult with the heavy rhythm of his snoring, had passed through all this unheeding, deep in the sleep of exhaustion.

The coast had soon settled back into the order of those long summer days: time passing was no more than the movement of the sun overhead, the irregular flurries of wings among a flotilla of drifting seabirds. For a while, a seal had lain in the offshore waters by Eilean na Rainich, its silky dog-like head aloof from the marauding bravado of some young herring gulls nearby. Slowly its head had swung round to get a full view of the coast and then, snout tilted, it had slipped unnoticed back into the deep water. Once or twice more it appeared along the coast and then was seen no more.

It was, in fact, in a moment of virtual silence that Murdo had woken. In spite of the pressures and anxieties of the night, he woke with a sense of well-being, with an inner warmth which followed his act of decision. But, at the same time, he woke with the dull and uncomfortable feeling of being trapped on Eilean na Rainich. He sat up and looked quickly around. Picking up his piece-bag and hobbling down to the water's edge, he had taken off his boots and socks and laid them out on a rock to dry. His stomach yawned with hunger and rooting around in his bag, he started to eat some bread and cheese, greedily chewing with an enormous circular motion of his jaw. Plucking the stalk off a leathery apple, he ate the whole fruit, core and all, wiped his mouth on the back of his hand and stared down at his feet. The flesh was wrinkled and white, spongy with dampness. As the heat from the warm rock and from the sun itself worked slowly into his tired body, he was gradually engulfed by a cloud of lethargy. The pool before him; the sunlight encasing him. He wandered unsteadily on the border of oblivion.

From behind Eilean na Rainich, a piercing whistle drove out into the air. Murdo sat bolt upright, staring out to sea, waiting for the sound to explain itself.

'Come here!'

A man's raucous voice called to a dog and then softened into conversation with somebody.

Leaving his things on the rock, Murdo got up slowly and, bending down, slid out of sight into the brackens.

At the near end of a long, narrow field that ran between the forest and the shore, Jimmie MacDonald, a middle-aged man who worked on the Dorusduan Estate, and a young lad up from the south and helping out for the summer months, prepared to finish off the fencing they had begun the day before. Jimmie's dog trotted around in intricate patterns, nose to the ground.

The two men started work, the younger one holding the stobs while the other hammered them into the ground with a mall. They worked in silence for a while, the only sound that of the mall's regular thud. Then the younger man offered to take a turn with the mall. Jimmie Mac-Donald looked at him briefly, smiled and, handing him the tool, picked up a stob. The Englishman swung the mall enthusiastically but without any great skill. He planted two stobs well enough but by the third the strain on his shoulders was beginning to tell and he struck two badly aimed blows. The third missed completely. Jimmie Mac-Donald, obviously ready for such an event, had his arm out of the way with great speed.

'Here now, you hold the stobs. It takes a while to get the feel of the mall.'

They started off again. The young man, determined not to show his annoyance, started to ask casual questions which Jimmie answered rather abruptly between blows of the mall.

'What was all that going on in Acheninver yesterday afternoon?'

'Oh that was Hughie's wedding. Him and Flora Munro.'

'Yes, but I heard there was a fire or something.'

'Aye . . . there was that.'

'But what happened?'

'Well, nobody rightly knows. It was the Munros' house.'

43

'No! But how did it start?'

'Well, it's hard to say.'

'Was anybody hurt?'

'No. At least, not so far as is known.'

'How do you mean? Anyway, I thought you were there yourself. At the wedding.'

'Aye, I was that.'

'And the house. Was it badly damaged?'

'Oh aye – bad enough so I hear. Margaret's having to stop with the Melvilles the while.'

'And what about him?'

'Who? Murdo? Oh, there's no telling . . . Come on now, we'll finish the row and then we'll need to be getting the tea.'

'OK. Are they going to call the police in though?'

'I couldn't rightly say.'

And with a final thud the last stob is planted in the ground before the massive straining-post and the men down their tools and head back to their piece-bags.

Across the glistening waters of the sound, the flap-eared head of Murdo Munro peered from the brackens. He stood half crouched, hands on knees, leaning forward and holding his breath as he tried to catch what Jimmie MacDonald was saying. But Jimmie MacDonald, though a friendly enough man with nothing against the Englishman, was not going to be drawn into committing himself by a stranger. So the talk went on about the estate and the work to be done; and all the while the Englishman never stopped questioning him about the island and its people. Jimmie MacDonald answered politely enough but never very precisely.

Murdo was just beginning to get uncomfortable when he heard Jimmie send the young man to fetch some staples. Jimmie watched him walk away across the field and then began to look out over the sea. For a moment, Murdo did

44

not realize what the man was doing and it was only when Jimmie shaded his eyes from the sun with his hand and looked in the direction of Eilean na Rainich that Murdo understood that he was not just looking but searching. Murdo stayed absolutely motionless while the man stared towards him. And then, as the young Englishman returned with the staples, Jimmie looked down and went back to drinking his tea.

Murdo sank slowly to his haunches and crawled away through the brackens until he had passed over the top of the little island and was in dead ground the other side. Only then did he stand up, walking quickly down to the shore to put on his socks and boots.

Jimmie MacDonald – or somebody else on the Dorus-duan Estate – must have noticed the boat missing from the Poll nam Morbh. Jimmie himself would not report it out of any vindictiveness; he would probably leave it for a day or two before mentioning it. But he might tell somebody if he thought that Murdo were in need of help. Once again Murdo realized that the sooner he left Eilean na Rainich the better.

All through that hot, timeless day Murdo waited on the seaward side of Eilean na Rainich for the two men to finish their work in the field. All day the peace of the coast was punctured by the dull blows of the mall and the tunings and gratings of the wire being pulled out and tautened. Murdo paced up and down the few feet of clear ground by the shore, kicking at stones and pulling at his rough chin with his hands. When he judged that it must soon be time for them to go home, he crept back into the brackens to watch them. And sure enough, not long afterwards, they began to collect their tools and prepared to leave. Twenty minutes later they had disappeared over the skyline and Murdo was once again alone.

He gathered all his things together and went down to

the boat. He would give the two men a while to get out of sight of the coast and then he would be off. During the hours of waiting he had decided that he would have to take the chance of being seen and row straight out for the mainland, cutting across the current far out where it was relatively weak.

He stood by the bows of the boat, tapping on the blade of one of the oars, on edge at having to wait these extra minutes. Finally he could stand it no longer. He slipped the rope from the boulder, climbed aboard and pushed off.

The sun still stood quite high in its afternoon quarter. The waters were calm, ruffled only by a light wind some way off the coast. The sea to the north was clear apart from a fishing boat way out on the horizon. Murdo felt his spirits lift. He reckoned that an hour and a half would find him on the mainland coast. He saw himself arriving, beaching the boat and slipping into the nearest village to buy himself a pie and a drink. He swallowed and bent his back into the oars, a look of determined anticipation on his face.

But a few minutes after putting out from Eilean na Rainich, he stopped and hung over the oars. In the middle of a stroke, he had glanced westwards along the coast beyond Am Bodha Ruadh. He stopped rowing, looked again and then seizing the oars, turned the boat and started to row at full speed back to the shore. When he reached Eilean na Rainich he rowed round into the sound behind the island and there he waited, sitting up straight and craning his neck to see over the rocks to the open sea.

A short while passed and then sleekly, silently, the shape of a large yacht came into sight, its steep prow splitting the water. Gradually her full length came into view as she slid unhurriedly along the coast. Murdo could make out the figure of a man at the helm. And then the yacht passed out of sight behind the island.

He rowed down to the other end of the sound and

46

waited to watch the yacht pass along the coast. A few minutes passed. A frown stretched across his forehead. Still the yacht did not appear. And then from the midst of the summer sea's silence rose the sound of voices followed by a clattering. The yacht had dropped anchor.

Murdo struck his knee and cursed. The hot, swelling frustration and anger rose violently in his stomach. He moved out from behind the island cautiously. The yacht lay about a hundred yards off Eilean na Rainich, its anchor chain a black root down into the water. He withdrew into the safety of the sound and sat, bent over the oars, prickling with exasperation. Below the boat, the sand was ridged with struts of black rock.

Some three or four hours later, shortly after sunset, with the sea's surface like a mass of writhing fish, Murdo Munro pulled his boat out from the sound and into the open sea. He had been watching the yacht for a while and now that the people on board had been below for some time, he thought that he had best make a run for it. To have waited much longer would have been to attempt most of the crossing in the dark.

The yacht lay against the glowing sky, its hull a form of simple elegance, its mast and rigging ink-drawn clear. A vague haze of light hovered about the cabin doorway. From time to time the sound of voices and laughter passed through the light and came across the water.

He rowed slowly but strongly, his arms taut with restrained effort. He aimed to pass on the landward side of the yacht. The oars dipped and pulled, dipped and pulled, sinking into the water with an oily succulence. The yacht lay five or six lengths off his port bow.

'Ahoy there!' A ripe, English voice hailed him.

Murdo turned guiltily and saw the silhouette of a man standing on deck with a hand on one of the stays. Taken unawares and confused by this rather nautical greeting, he could not find the right answer.

47

'Oh, hullo,' he said with a forced casualness. 'It's a fine evening.'

'Superb. First-rate. You wouldn't have any lobsters for sale by any chance, would you?'

'Lobsters? Och no, not me . . .'

'Oh. Thought you might be one of the lobster boys . . .'

The black shape of the man put down his glass and fumbled for a cigarette. The little spurt of flame from the lighter showed a fatty, reddish face. Murdo drifted along not knowing what to do. Half at a loss for what to say, half because a vague idea had suddenly slipped into his mind, he spoke again.

'You'll have come quite a way today.'

'What? No, not really. Wasn't enough wind most of the time. We heard on the radio that there's going to be a good breeze from the south-west tomorrow so we were hoping to push on north; but unfortunately my wife's gone and hurt her wrist so we'll have to give it a rest for a day or two.'

'Will you be thinking of going far?'

'Dunno. All depends on the weather, you know. Should like to try and get out to Lewis eventually, but no definite plans . . . Are you just out for an evening paddle, eh?'

'No, not really . . . Seeing how it was a fine evening I was thinking I'd try my luck with the fish. I stay back up there.' Murdo made a suitably vague gesture towards the forest.

'Nice and peaceful, I should think. Caught anything?'

'No, not much . . . And where'll you be thinking of going to from here?'

'Oh, just thataway.' The man waved towards the north. 'It's no good planning ahead too much on holiday.'

'No, you're right there . . .' Murdo replied and then added quietly, as if an afterthought, 'I've to go north myself.'

48

'Have you? Off on holiday, eh?'

'Aye, well, in a way. I've to go away up and see my sister. I'm wanting away tomorrow but I'll need to wait until Monday for there's no ferry tomorrow, it being a Sunday.'

'Oh, I see.' A silence which Murdo did not try to break. 'Listen, I don't suppose you'd care to come north with us, would you? You see, I'd like to make the best of the wind tomorrow so I could do with some help. Are you any good on one of these?'

'Well, I can't say I've had much experience really.'

'Oh, you'd soon get the hang of it! What do you say?'

'Well . . . aye, it would suit me just fine.'

'Good! Look, I'll just tell my wife. Darling!'

A woman's tall shape appeared beside him.

'Darling, Mr . . . Excuse me, I don't think I got your name,' he said, turning back to Murdo.

'Oh – it's Mackenzie. Archie Mackenzie.'

'Mr Mackenzie is wanting to go north so I've asked him if he'll give us a hand for a day or two till your wrist's better. We can put him down on the coast wherever's convenient for him.'

'That's very good of you, Mr Mackenzie. Darling, how marvellous!' Her voice was full of jaded enthusiasm.

'Look, we'd like to leave about eightish tomorrow morning. Would that suit you?'

'Aye, that'd be fine.'

'Good, well that's that . . . I tell you what – take our rubber dinghy back with you now so that you can get out here in the morning. OK?'

'Right you are. Well, I'd best be on my way now before the light's gone.'

And the little rubber dinghy is attached to the stern of Murdo's boat and he is pulling away into the rising darkness.

'Goodnight, Mr Mackenzie. See you tomorrow.'

'Aye. Goodnight.'

The English couple go below leaving only the gush of light from the cabin doorway as a pennant of comfort and security fixed on the field of darkness. Murdo hears the muffled noise of the rubber dinghy slipping over his wake. The handles of the wooden oars are smooth and warm against his palms. The rowlocks creak gently in a rhythm crossing that of the ripples tapping at the bows. He pauses for a moment, immensely calm, and looks up at the stars, suddenly aware of the expanding peace about him. The wind skims his ragged face. Before him the sea extends hidden and unknown: all around and above stands the dark pelt of the night sky. Only the shelving declivity of the coast behind him, dimly visible, is a reminder of the past.

Murdo stayed there a while longer, thinking over the lucky outcome of his meeting with the couple on the yacht. Then the moon, until now trapped behind a bank of evening cloud, broke clear and began to climb out across the sky. It woke Murdo from his trance and in the wash of new light he rowed back to Eilean na Rainich. He went round into the sound, beached the boat on the shore below the field and then crossed the sound again in the rubber dinghy. Back in his cave, he ate all the food remaining in his piece-bag. The moon retreated behind the clouds again. The light on the yacht hung in the darkness for a while and then, suddenly, was gone. Half an hour later Murdo was sound asleep.

He awoke early the next morning. The day had broken bright and sunny but with a good wind blowing up behind the island, flocks of puffy clouds drove across the sky. Offshore, just beyond where the yacht lay, the sea ran with small waves.

He had no watch but reckoned by the sun that it must be

around six o'clock. He wished he had not finished all his food the night before. Moving into the cover of the brackens, he sat and watched the yacht. For about an hour there was no sign of life and then the man appeared, walking round the deck, stretching and looking out to sea. A short while later he went below again. Murdo waited fifteen minutes or so and then, collecting his things for the last time, crossed the island to the dinghy. He rowed leisurely out of the sound. When he got to the yacht he could see nobody so he rapped half-heartedly on the hull. The man's head appeared round the cabin doorway.

'Good morning, Mr Mackenzie. Come along aboard.'

And Murdo clambers aboard and as he sets foot on the deck feels himself already safe. He looks back to Eilean na Rainich and the island beyond.

'Darling, give Mr Mackenzie a cup of tea, will you? I just want to have a look at the charts.'

Murdo looks at the man. In his early forties, heavily built, fatty-faced, with grizzled hair. Kind, green eyes.

'Why don't you go below, Mr Mackenzie. I'll be with you in a jiffy.'

'Oh . . . right you are.'

And Murdo treads his way gingerly down the steps to the cabin where he finds a woman seated by a table with the remains of breakfast before her. She is younger. Tall, elegant, bird-featured, smooth sallow skinned, indolent. Her eyes have that look of self-assurance that Murdo connects with visitors from the south. As she raises a cigarette to her mouth he notices that her wrist is bandaged. The cabin is simply decorated but is both roomy and comfortable. Not knowing where to put himself and unable to look the woman in the face, Murdo hovers, ill at ease.

'Do sit down, Mr Mackenzie. Would you like some tea?'

'Oh . . . aye, I would that.'

He sits on the edge of a chair, takes the cup from the

woman, adds five lumps of sugar and drinks. His face puckers slightly for the tea is strange, weak and scented compared to that which he normally drinks. His stomach empty, he tries to keep his eyes off the toast and butter on the table. The woman starts to make polite conversation. Murdo finds her clipped accent difficult to understand. He answers her courteously but remotely. But all the while his mind is taken up by the great feeling of safety which he has. He is enclosed in the comforts of the womb-like cabin, about to leave his old life, the scene of his defeat, about to travel away north, disguised, protected by the money of these people. He, Murdo Munro, who for all these years had lived in Acheninver, resigned, sullen, working hard so as not to think, here he was, setting out to sea on his way to a new life . . . It was hard to know what the meaning of it all was. Anyway, so long as he was away from Margaret – that was what mattered.

And it was in thinking this that he came to realize that his feeling for Margaret was not one of mere indifference as he had told himself all these years. He had told himself this because it was the only way of bearing the strain of their relationship: his feeling for her, in fact, was one of hatred. He hated her for the way she had played him into marrying her. He hated her for having made him live the life he had. But he hated her most of all for turning his Flora against him. Murdo was not a hard man but there was suddenly no place in his heart for compassion for Margaret. No, she had got what she deserved . . .

'Mr Mackenzie . . .'

And whatever happened as a result of his burning the house, he would never go back to her. No, never . . .

'Mr Mackenzie. Would you like some more tea?'

'Och, I'm sorry. I was dreaming. No, I won't, thank you very much. That was just fine.'

And then the man reappeared and they went on deck

and prepared to set sail. Murdo had had no sailing experience and was quite at a loss as to what to do. But the man was patient and gave instructions and explained himself; and a short while later the yacht came round and began to pull away from the coast. For a moment the sails flapped but then they tautened and the water rolled and then bubbled and hissed its way along the hull. By the time Murdo remembered to look back, Eilean na Rainich could no longer be distinguished from the main island.

With the wind almost dead behind them, there was little for Murdo to do once they were under way. To begin with, he stayed near the man, feeling that he should show willing; and they had a kind of unenthusiastic conversation. The man, obviously passionate about little except sailing, really wanted to talk about that; but was unable to raise much response from Murdo who regarded all boats as a form of either transport or livelihood. So the conversation lapsed and the man began to smoke a pipe while Murdo perched beside him. Eventually the woman came on deck and the couple soon fell into a conversation of boats and friends and other things far removed from Murdo's life. So he wandered off and sat on a coil of rope and stared over the sea to the high-backed islands that were coming down to meet them.

They passed out round the bulge of the mainland to which Murdo had originally been heading and then left the coast to cut through the islands. The boat dipped and sprang, the rigging fretted by the wind, the sails swollen hard, the spray rising in thin sheets sown with sunlight. Murdo watched the coast slowly unfolding itself. But then, suddenly, his good spirits fell. His release from Acheninver and then Eilean na Rainich and the first moments aboard the yacht had kept his mind tense and alert. But now that his safety grew more assured every

53

mile the yacht sailed from the island, he found himself faced by the uncertainty of his future.

He would go to his sister Bessie and tell her what had happened. Aye, well, tell her that he had left Margaret at any rate. He would stop with her a while and perhaps give her a hand with the croft. And, well, see how things turned out. Perhaps he could find work in the district . . . In any case, Bessie would know best what to do. And so his mind coiled off into the vagaries of his imagination.

For years he had had to take no decisions, make no arrangements; for Margaret had liked to organize everything. And even his work in the forest had been a routine. So now that he was to make his own plans his ideas were often distorted and self-centred. It was not that there was anything wilfully selfish in him but it was the kind of self-centred imbalance of a person used to living in a world of his own. The problems at home had cut him off, had given him a crusty exterior so that people who did not know him well were often wary, fearing the sharpness of his tongue. At the same time those few who had got to know him better saw that he was basically kind, a man who would be the first to spring to the aid of somebody in difficulties. The men at work, long inured to his outward bitterness, would purposely provoke him and laugh to hear him curse and grumble. But this was done without malice. Murdo knew this and reacted as he did, partly because it brought him relief. It was a satisfactory process of drawing the sting. But in spite of the pressures within him, Murdo never opened himself to anybody. It was not, in any case, a tendency of the island people with their small, interwoven communities; but even less so was it for Murdo.

Yet even before his marriage Murdo had shown signs of withdrawal, of remoteness from other people. He had been born the second of two children to an Acheninver fisherman. Willie Munro had been a large, dark-skinned man with a dry sense of humour and a passion for his wife. Mairi, also from the village, had loved her man well. She had been of average height, lightly built, with dark brown hair and a rather gaunt face from which her clear blue eyes had stared forth with a mixture of calmness and concern. And it had been something of a joke among the people of Acheninver how Willie Munro worshipped his woman. Indeed Murdo himself remembered the way in which his father had been used to sit over his tea in the kitchen while his mother wandered about talking all the while. Willie Munro had sat there chewing his food, putting in a word here and there but never taking his eyes off his woman.

Murdo's sister, Bessie, had been born three years before him. She had grown into a quiet but singularly strong-willed girl with her father's dark features and her mother's build. Murdo, always an ungainly, moody child had looked up in admiration to his pretty and competent sister. From an early age he had followed her about and wanted to join in with her friends rather than play with the other small boys of the village. It was about the age of nine that he suddenly started to ignore Bessie, now a girl of twelve, and began to hang around the house, sulky and difficult. As he grew older he had one or two good friends in the village but always seemed unwilling to join in with the gatherings of the Acheninver boys. He never quite lost this moodiness and gradually became something of a solitary, going off on long rambles by himself and giving his mother only vague answers as to where he had been.

Murdo's father, like other of the local men, had been away to the Great War. But when he came back, the family soon picked up its old routines. The fishing had its ups and downs, giving Mairi her days and nights of anxiety. But all this was a commonplace in every fisherman's family and the Munros survived and were a happy home with the large man as the figurehead and the blue-eyed woman as the quiet ruling force.

And then one day, when Murdo was nearly eighteen and newly started as a farmhand with Johnnie Totaig, Willie Munro's boat failed to come home with the others of the fleet. It had been wild all night and the dim winter's morning had come to show a black-green sea everywhere thrashed into foam. All the other boats were in, but for a while everybody remained optimistic. All morning Murdo worked hard, trying to keep his eyes from the sea. By midday the coastguards had been alerted and a full-scale search was organized. The following morning, after a long-drawn night during which Mairi and the two children had lain in their beds with open, staring eyes, the news came through that bits of wreckage had been sighted about ten miles off the Rubha na Sgarbh on the south-west coast of the island. It was nothing definite, of course, and there was still room for hope. For three days the young man and the two women waited, without hope, silently, praying for an end to the uncertainty. And then the body of young Calum Southern, one of the boys on the boat, was washed ashore and there was no further room for doubt. The bodies of the other men were never recovered.

Murdo had gone back to work with a dull fury biting into his soul, the fury of a young man abruptly made aware of his powerlessness in the face of circumstance. In some illogical way it was the fact that he had not known of his father's going till many hours after his death that harried Murdo so. He, Murdo, healthy and strong, had been sleeping in his bed as his father's boat, toiling into heavy seas, had topped a wave and gone sliding, sliding on down into a gigantic trough from which she had never risen. Perhaps this was how it had been. Perhaps, and here again was the pain, the pain without cure. He had heard the fishermen talk of the winter seas out in the

Minch; talk of how a combination of wind and wave could open up freak troughs, like holes, all of sixty feet deep, into which the hardiest fishing boat would plunge without hope of coming up again. He had seen, too, boats come home with their bridgework smashed, simply driven backwards by the blow from one large wave. And it was now, as he went about his work on the farm, that all these details, previously accepted as part of his father's work, came forward to form a hideous picture of the boat's foundering, his father's last seconds, the darkness, the isolation, the gasping and the thunderous foam.

And Johnnie Totaig, coming round the corner of the byre, had found Murdo turned to the wall, his face in his hands, his shoulders shaking uncontrollably. The old bachelor had taken the boy into his kitchen, talking to him as he would to an animal in pain, his great twisted hands patting the boy's arm, and had fed him a tumbler of whisky before sending him home. Back in Acheninver, a silence filled the house but otherwise the three of them went about their lives much as before. In this way a dignity of pride was preserved and if either Mairi or Bessie wept it was under cover of darkness while the rest of Acheninver slept.

The weeks passed and slowly the family's wound began to heal. Mairi managed to get herself a part-time job helping in the big house at Salachy, up the glen; Bessie went on as before, working as a receptionist in a hotel in the island's main town; while Murdo, after staying another six or seven months with Johnnie Totaig, got a job working in the forest belonging to the Salachy Estate, up on the hills behind the house where his mother worked.

And so the Munro household remained until the following autumn, nearly a year after Willie Munro's death. Bessie had come home one evening looking dark and strained and when Murdo returned from having a pint in the Acheninver Hotel, he found his mother and sister deep in conversation in the kitchen. It was with a forced delight that Mairi told Murdo that Bessie was soon to be married. It was forced, firstly, because the suddenness of the announcement was due to the fact that Bessie had found herself pregnant; and, secondly, because the man in question was an East Coast man called Willie Noble who had a small farm halfway between Acheninver and the town but who was disliked for the attentions he paid to other men's wives. But none of this was said amongst the three of them and they celebrated quietly, trying to make the best of what was clearly an unsatisfactory match. In the event, however, things turned out quite otherwise. Some time after the wedding Bessie suffered a miscarriage; while Willie Noble proved himself to be a most considerate – and faithful – husband.

With Bessie married and away, Murdo felt even more of a duty towards his mother. In her married life she had not felt a great need for other people; and somehow, after her man was gone, she could no longer find it in herself to start up new friendships. It was as if this side of her had been drained. So that, apart from her working hours, Mairi spent most of her time alone unless Murdo was with her. Whether Murdo ended by stopping at home out of loyalty to his mother or as an excuse to avoid mixing with the others in the hotel, would have been hard to say: but stop at home he did.

Three years passed uneventfully. Three years made up of the unchanging cycle of seasons, of day after day of work punctuated by the small joys of family gatherings. And then the war came. At the call-up, Murdo failed his medical and finally got sent to work in a canteen up towards the Butt of Lewis. He and the others out there suffered little from the war. They managed well enough, eating at the canteen, and now and then adding to their diet by shooting wild swan and duck. At the end of the war he returned to Acheninver to find his mother quite unchanged but many of the local men dead or missing. One of these was Willie Noble who had stepped on a land mine eight months before he was due to come home. After struggling on for a while with a farm that had been on the decline for some years, Bessie sold up and came back to Acheninver.

For a while Bessie seemed unable to adjust to her widowhood. She worked here and there and smiled nicely enough to people when they spoke to her but, like her mother after Willie's death, her enthusiasm for the business of living seemed to have gone. But there was nothing to be done, so both Mairi and he waited in the hope that she would marry again. She was just thirty and a fine-looking girl. It was only a matter of time.

There was a woman, some years younger than Mairi, called Isa McKenzie. She had been a friend of both Mairi and Bessie but in the first years of the war had left Acheninver to marry a man called Johnnie Matheson who lived up on the far north-west coast of the mainland. From time to time she had written to Mairi, in the knowledge that she led a lonely life, and so they had kept in touch. Not long after the war, Isa hearing from Mairi that Bessie was in poor spirits, invited the girl to come and stay for a while. Both Mairi and Murdo urged her to go and so finally she accepted. She stayed there five or six weeks, helping in the shop that Johnnie owned and when she came back to Acheninver, she was much changed.

A few weeks later Mairi heard from Isa that Johnnie's elder brother, Duncan, was to be on the island for a day or two and asked if he might come and visit the Munros. This was soon arranged but it was only an hour or so before Duncan was expected that Mairi, seeing Bessie carefully dressed and rather silent, realized what was going to happen. And sure enough, Duncan arrived, a large-boned man in his middle forties with bright eyes and a habit of wrinkling his nose as he spoke; and in a moment when both Mairi and Murdo were out of the room, he managed to ask Bessie to marry him. She accepted. And so it was that, once again, Bessie left Acheninver, this time to go a hundred and twenty miles due north to Duncan's croft at Camascoille near the village of Drienach.

Mairi always promised to go and visit Bessie. And indeed three years later she had finally made arrangements to go north and spend Hogmanay with the Mathesons. But in the midst of preparing the house for her mother's arrival, Bessie had received a telegram from Murdo saying that Mairi had taken a heart attack and was being kept in hospital. Four weeks later she was dead and Murdo found himself alone in the family house in Acheninver.

It was to be only a month or so after his mother's death, in the winter of his thirty-third year that he took shelter under that black overhang of rock with Margaret Allen from Selkirk and so set in motion the slow decline of his life. Mainly under pressure from Margaret, he had sold the family home and the newly married couple had moved into the council house to which Murdo was to set fire twenty-six years later.

He stared morosely into the water that tumbled and sluiced along the smooth-faced hull of the yacht and wondered where this ceaseless progression, in which he was never quite sure whether he was hunter or hunted, was to end. And leaning right forward to peer over the side into the green-deep waters of the sea, he wondered too if he had not perhaps already lived long enough.

CHAPTER FOUR

The room was small and in the grey light it was not possible to make out more than the barest outlines of an old chest of drawers, a small wardrobe, a chair and a narrow bed in which a woman lay asleep. The bed was against the wall and on the other side of the room the ceiling sloped downwards, following the line of the roof into which was set a dormer window. The silence was total though broken regularly by the sound of the sleeper breathing.

Within the next half-hour, the room began to shed its two-dimensional masking so that every moment new details slipped forward into focus as the light outside gradually grew. The room which slowly revealed itself had been furnished purely with regard to practical necessities so that there was little in the way of superfluous decoration except a small model horse made of straw which perched precariously on a ledge beneath the window. On the bed-side table was a frame containing a faded picture of a man dressed in a suit, looking sternly out over the bed into the distance. For all the formality of his pose there was a covert humour in his bright eyes. Thirty-five years earlier the frame had held the photograph of another man; but this was neither here nor there for both of them were now dead.

The sunlight, growing in strength, cut a band of yellow-ing brightness across the middle of the bed. The woman moved slightly, compressing her lips for a moment and then fell backwards again into the complex folds of sleep that fill the last hours before waking. Her grey hair was pulled back from her face into a small bun. This, with her prominent cheekbones and the sharp ridge to her nose, gave her face a harshness out of keeping with her character. But her mouth, formed without trace of either grossness or acrimony, could have been an outward sign of her inner calm and open-mindedness. The skin of her eyelids was polished almost to transparency and showed up the minute forkings of veins.

Bessie Matheson, asleep in her widow's bed at the age of sixty-one, could fairly have been described as a good woman.

As the bar of sunlight from between the curtains moved up across the bed towards her face, Bessie began to shift about, her forehead wrinkling, as if in protest at the day that was pulling her from her sleep. Then twice her eyelids lifted for a second and her blue eyes looked uncomprehendingly out from her sleep into the waking world; and twice they closed again as she tried to follow the receding thread of a dream. Even when she was finally awake, she lay with her eyes still shut, caught in the process of preparing for the coming day. Her thoughts passed backwards and forwards, touching at the many things she wanted to get done. But behind all this, there was something else, something lying like a dead weight across her consciousness, something unsolved carried forward from the day before. Across the expanses of a few empty seconds her mind ranged; and then, abruptly, she remembered that the day before, the postman had come with a letter for her from Walter MacFarlane, the minister at Acheninver.

And a strange letter it was. The minister started by explaining that, two days before, he had married her niece, Flora Munro to Hughie Morrison in the kirk at Acheninver. Well, this she had known well enough and had indeed sent a present for the couple. From that point onwards the letter had become a bit vague, speaking of something which he several times referred to as 'the tragedy' and saying that nobody quite knew where Murdo was. He said that he thought Murdo was a fine man, that he was sure that he had not meant any harm and that if he should come to Camascoille, would she be so kind as to try to persuade him to get in touch with him. He was sure that he and Murdo would be able to sort everything out. At the top of the letter the telephone number had been underlined in green ink.

Bessie had not known what to make of the letter. She had not seen Murdo in twelve years; from the time when she had gone to visit him and Margaret. Even then, anyone could have seen that they were not happy. But they had managed all right and, well, after that many years of marriage you would hardly expect a person to get up and walk out . . . No, there was no sense in it at all. And if Murdo had left, would he come to Camascoille? Aye, Bessie thought he might well do that.

She opened her eyes and glanced towards the window. A while before she need be up. And as she looked away, the man's bright eyes caught her notice. It was close on fourteen years since Duncan had died that hot autumn night. Her memory fell open and she saw down the many years of her widow's life. When he had gone it had been bad in many ways; but she did not grieve. When Willie, her first husband, was killed the pain had left her feeble for many months. But there had been a strangeness in her first marriage, mainly because the last four years of it had been in the war with Willie home on leave for a few days and then away again for long and indefinite periods, so that his presence was always connected with the panic of pleasure. Otherwise, dreams had been her subsistence: dreams of how they would get the farm going again, how they would be happy and forget, how . . . And then the telegram had arrived and for a long while she had wished that it had been her who had died.

When Duncan had asked her to marry him, it had been a relief to join somebody else's life, with its problems, and so to cast away those of her own. Duncan with his slow, half-fatherly ways, with that strange laughter in his eyes which suggested that he was unable to take either himself or life seriously. It seemed to her that her hope returned as soon as Duncan first made her laugh. And so it had been for the fifteen years of their marriage – a companionship that had found its greatest strength in the man's ability to buoy them both with his laughter. And after she had turned over in their great creaking bed that hot, silent night and found him already dead, Bessie had grieved but without despair.

The bolt of sunlight was fixed deep into the pillow beside her head. She stretched slowly, tentatively, exploring the ache in her back. Then, slipping out of bed, she began to dress.

In the other bedroom, across the landing, Mary Matheson heard her walk across the room to the cupboard. She, too, had also been awake for some time. She had lain there quite still in the bed and gazed vacantly at the corner of the mantelpiece, wondering if she would ever get the better of her husband's drinking. She was thirty and though she was not fat, every part of her small body was rounded. Her hair was red and coarse, her face freckled, her nose dumpy. Her eyes, grey-green, seemed small and insignificant in her face, perhaps from the very lightness of her eyelashes. It was only Mary's closest friends who ever told her she looked pretty.

A heavy knee bumped into the back of her thigh as her husband moved slowly upwards from the darker levels of sleep. Two years older than Mary, Alec was a man of solid proportions. His hair was black and as rough as heather roots, his eyes green and his face usually covered with the stubble of a three-day beard. His hands, massively powerful, now lay locked together on the pillow by his chin.

Johnnie Matheson, in whose shop in Drienach Bessie had helped after the war, had been some eighteen months younger than his brother. On their father's death the croft at Camascoille had gone to Duncan, partly as the elder son, partly because Johnnie had already established his shop in the village. Johnnie and Isa had run the shop successfully; and, rather late in their marriage, Alec had been born to them. When Alec was sixteen, his father died and since he had no interest in the shop he let his mother sell it. Isa went from time to time to help Bessie out at Camascoille. Alec, in the meantime, had gone away to Glasgow where he laboured for a year or two and then joined the Merchant Navy. Two winters later, while he was in the Mediterranean off North Africa, the whole west coast of Scotland fell under a short spell of hard frosts and bitter winds. In this weather Isa caught the flu, neglected herself and took a bad attack of pneumonia. Her health had never been too strong and she failed to recover fully from this illness, lasting just long enough for Alec to reach home in answer to Bessie's telegram.

With the house in Drienach now his, Alec thought of coming home for good. But the life at sea had given him ideas that made the prospects of staying in a West Highland village seem unappealing. So he put the house up for sale and went back to join his ship, frittering away both the money from his mother and from the sale of the house. Nine months after he had returned to sea, Duncan died at Camascoille. Three and a half years had seen both Matheson brothers and one of their wives die. Bessie was left with the croft.

It seemed a raw prospect for Bessie to try and run the croft alone and she remembered the months on the farm after Willie had died. But up at Drienach it was somehow different. It was, perhaps that the crofts around Drienach were much nearer to each other, a more compact community. For once she had buried Duncan and was back at Camascoille, there always seemed to be people offering to lend a hand. At first Bessie thought that this was just a way of helping her in her widow's grief; but as the months went by, it continued and there slowly evolved an unspoken rota, an unacknowledged routine so that most days of the week there would be somebody over to give her some help. She did what little she could in return. It was never really enough but nobody thought of it in that way and the gesture was received.

And so six more years had passed.

And then it was that Alec, after his years at sea, came back to Drienach. Nobody quite knew why: indeed he had scarcely been expected, having sold the family home that while ago. But he said that he had had enough of the sea, enough wandering. He had neither work nor place to stay when he came back and only a little money. And he was drinking. For a few nights he slept on the sofa of an old friend and then, one afternoon early in the spring, he walked out the three miles or so to Camascoille. Bessie stood at the kitchen window and watched him come across the open land with that inimitable walk of his, shoulders hunched, hands in pockets and eyes on the ground and had wondered what she would say to him when he asked her.

Well, he had taken a cup of tea with her and had been quiet and reticent for all his rough ways. And then, abruptly, he said that she must be needing help on the croft and perhaps he could start working it with her. He said it in a sort of insolent, presumptuous way but Bessie had not held it against him for she saw his shyness and was pleased that this rough-necked boy should be coming back to the family croft. And so, slowly, over the empty tea-cups it was all arranged. Though Alec would be out to Camascoille every day, he would be finding himself a room in the village for the while.

Alec worked hard, the croft did well and the arrangement seemed to suit them both. But Alec was not happy. He was cheerful enough with Bessie but sometimes, when he did not know that he was being watched, Bessie would see him pause in his work and stare out to sea. And she heard, too, that he was forever getting himself into trouble in the village. That he drank, she knew. But what she learnt was that the drink had the effect of releasing an anger in him that usually got him into a brawl and trouble with the police. When he came out to Camascoille with his face puffy and grey, his eyes red-rimmed, Bessie would try to shame him with his drinking. She spoke calmly yet firmly but he just stood there sullen with guilt or annoyance and would not answer. After a time she gave up.

But about a year after he returned to Drienach, he got himself married to Mary Tindal, the daughter of the local coalman. At Bessie's suggestion, the young couple came to live out at Camascoille. Bessie found Mary an easy companion; and she also realized that Mary was the one person who seemed to be able to put some restraint on Alec's drinking. Indeed for a month or two after they arrived at Camascoille, he stopped drinking altogether.

However, they soon realized that the croft would not support the three of them. So Alec went and took a job working on the roads with the Council, working the croft in his spare time. He would leave the house soon after seven in the morning, walking the mile and a half to the road-end from where he got a lift into the village. He got home in the same manner to begin with; but one day he arrived back much later, saying that he had missed his lift and had had to walk the whole way. And, of course, it was only a matter of time before this became a routine, with him creeping in at all hours and mumbling thin excuses and his voice fogged with the drink.

At first, Mary made light of it. Then she had become silent in her anger; and, finally, Bessie saw what was coming and made herself scarce. She went to bed early and lay there in the dark unable to sleep. At last she heard Alec's steps outside the house and the back door closing quietly. Then the voices had started, low but insistent to begin with but finally breaking out into shouts of uncontrolled anger.

But soon after, the problem was brought to a head when one of the men from the Council chose to come over to Drienach on an unannounced tour of inspection. Alec, with a few drinks on him, chanced to be by the road when the car appeared. One of the others quickly tried to hustle him out of the way but Alec, losing his temper, turned and knocked the man to the ground. At the end of the week, he was given his books.

It was with a degree of relief that Mary and Bessie had him back at Camascoille. He still managed to get away to his drinking but the bad days were rare so Mary left him to them. Meanwhile, she took a job in Drienach instead, which she held until the beginning of the following summer when she was within a month of having her first child. In those last few weeks of her pregnancy, life was good at Camascoille with Mary exuberant and Alec both sober and attentive. In the bright warmth of early June she was taken in to the district hospital where she gave birth to a boy.

After she had come home, the peace at Camascoille continued. Alec was quiet and always willing to help, rarely went out drinking and, when he did, managed to come home reasonably sober. It was only Bessie, who had seen such things before, who watched pleased but apprehensive.

And she was right, for this state of peace was short-lived. The strand of restlessness, of bitterness against his own circumstances, was a deep-rooted part of Alec's character. It could be smothered for a while but there was never any doubt that it would eventually break out again. And so it did, with him slowly returning to his drinking habits and with the violent scenes between him and Mary becoming more and more frequent, he fierce with guilt, she driven by shame and worry.

But, in spite of all this, the young boy, Dougie, grew up into a sturdy, well-balanced child appearing to be totally impervious to the regular battles that raged about him. Often Bessie, seeing the beginning of trouble between Alec and Mary, would get the boy away into the other room. When Mary felt the boy was old enough to be left with Bessie, she went back to her job in Drienach. And again the Mathesons, old and young, settled back into their lives.

Dougie grew fast and by the time he was seven he had turned into a wiry boy, with a thatch of brown hair and large, prune-coloured eyes. He spent all his time out with his father and the dogs or loose about the countryside, alone, coming home for his tea with his clothes ripped and crusted with mud.

And so things were at Camascoille when Murdo Munro came ashore from the yacht some fifteen miles down the coast from Drienach. They had come up from the south before a good wind, spending the nights in small bays and passing only occasional boats as they sailed.

Murdo and the English couple had been uneasy together. Murdo, perhaps more accustomed to long silences, was not as disconcerted by the lagging conversation as were the man and his wife. In the evenings, when the drink was brought out, they both relaxed: while Murdo sat on the edge of his chair, sipping at his glass like a child, unable to enjoy his whisky. The couple lost some of their formality after a few drinks and became both confused and patronizing, telling Murdo how fine his country was and how he ought to be proud of it. Murdo smiled and agreed politely, wondering why they were telling him this. And so, once again, the conversation fell into silence and later, when he was in his bunk, Murdo wondered to himself what it was that made these English townsfolk so strange. It seemed to him that he understood the things they said; and yet, at the same time, he often could not understand their reasons for saying them. It was as if they had all the education and clever speech without any common sense to go with it.

One afternoon they anchored near the coast and the man rowed Murdo ashore in the dinghy. By the time Murdo had reached the top of the beach, the man was back at the yacht. Murdo turned and vanished from sight into a great thicket of gorse.

Deep in the gorse he found a small clearing where the grass was soft and smooth and from where he could see out to a road that passed by half a mile inland.

He sat down and was immediately aware of the sun's heat, obliquely shining, on his neck. The sea winds that had covered him all morning were nowhere to be felt and after the days away from land, he was sharply conscious of the rich, earthy smells about him. The gorse, the turf, the heathers and brackens, all close by, lay under the palm of the heat; while, drifting from further away, came strands of smells off the bog-myrtle and the spreading township of peat-hags that filled the slopes between him and the road. And through the entanglement of these smells was threaded the sharpness of the salt.

Some wheatears moved busily about a patch of grass

below him; a passing skylark called liquidly; somewhere out of sight a stonechat sounded harsh and indignant. Murdo felt himself being drawn forward into a warm forest of sleep. He lay back on the grass with his hands beneath his head and stared blindly into the vitreous blue above. For a moment he saw the sky and the branches of the pine trees on the ridge above Acheninver; but then it passed and his eyes closed. The small but persistent sounds around him gradually slipped into the distance, his mouth and throat became sweet and heavy and then the last edge of his consciousness was finally covered. A few minutes later, the wheatears that had been foraging on the grass below, fluttered up and landing close by the sleeping man, began to hunt for insects.

The sun moved on across the sky. The sheep beyond the road grazed for a while longer and then lay down in the afternoon heat. Birds arrived and settled, called a few times and moved on in their ceaseless journeying. Bees and insects droned and gruzzed in the heavy folds of the air around the gorse bushes. The brightness of water in a patch of peat-moss sparkled tirelessly. And the surface of the baked peat cracked constantly wider. Occasionally, a solitary car, small and lost in the spreading land, passed with a muted growl along the stretch of road and vanished behind the hill. Like the backwash of a wave, the flood of silence ran in again upon the land.

It was about two hours later, when a passing car sounded its horn at a sheep, that Murdo awoke. He looked around sleepily for a moment and then sat up. He watched the car disappear out of sight, yawned, stretched and looked up at the sun. Realizing how long he must have been asleep, he quickly gathered up his belongings and, hurrying down the slope, made off across the peat-hags in the direction of the road. The small head with the thin greasy hair rose and fell, vanished and reappeared in the deep pits of the peat; but finally he came forth and, reaching the road, turned to the north. He walked away quickly and had soon passed out of sight.

Within minutes of his disappearing, the slow heavy beat of a lorry was to be heard toiling gently up from the south. It eventually came into view, lumbered sleepily along the straight and was gone. Across the still air it could be heard labouring on for a short way and then the pitch of the sound fell and was cut off. The bright, flat noise of a door being slammed and the slow, climbing rumble as the lorry got under way again was heard before this sound, too, was swallowed up in the silence.

Seated high in the lorry's cab, Murdo watched the landscape unfolding before him as they ground and turned their way northwards along the coast. They skirted small bays of clear sand where oystercatchers and ringed plovers stood dotted by the surf. The sunlight glinted off the sea and the hard polish of the wet sand; while higher on the beach everything was dry whiteness and heat with sandflies and rock burning smooth. And then suddenly this was past as the lorry cut in from the coast and started to haul up a long slope with the hinterland ahead spreading immense and empty, heat quivering before the mountains. They stood in the haze with layer upon layer of buttress and flank and dull dark walls of rock, all drained of colour and depth by the long hours beneath the sun.

The heavily loaded lorry crawled upwards and on through the rolling desert of heathers and rock, the occasional puff of sea air noticeably cool in the heat of the cab. For moments, all sight of the mountains was lost as the road twisted and turned in the pleats in its search for the higher ground. The engine roared monotonously, small cliff-faces passed within reach of the window, glass-fluting burns thrust their way beneath the road, tall brackens arched motionless in the dead heat, a hoodie watched from the branches of a rotten tree. Still the thin band of tarmac coiled upwards ahead.

But the lorry followed it stubbornly and finally, with a last roar, it broke free of the rocky gorge and came out into the clear airs and spaces of a rolling plateau. The lower slopes of the mountains were now no more than a mile away and although the sea lay hidden from view its coolness breathed in steadily from across the peaty ground. Ringed by a low dyke of hills, the plateau was a world apart and the road drove unbending across its middle. Crossing low over the landscape, the high-winged form of a hen-harrier hunted lazily in the heat.

Murdo sat leaning forwards peering all around. Compared to the island landscape, it seemed strangely different. It was perhaps both the greater spaces and the rougher surface of the ground that gave him the sensation of being far out in wilderness. For the combination of slab rock and open grasses, which covered much of the island, was here to be seen only on the higher ground, on the mountain flanks. While the rolling ground between the mountains and the sea was an unbridled mass of rock, wildly knotted and rough. It was as if the ground were everywhere encrusted with barnacles.

Reaching the plateau's far edge, the road dropped and once again took up its eel-like route among the rocks in its attempts to reach down to the sea. The lorry's weight urged it on with insistence and the engine roared and raced in its efforts to restrain it. Like a great cumbersome beast, it lowered itself down the slopes and came out by a long beach where rock and sand were marked with the bright bursts of holidaymakers. And then this too was past and once again they were setting out across tracts of emptiness.

It was already late in the afternoon when Murdo stood at the turning and watched the lorry pulling away on the road to the north. He settled his piece-bag and thornproof over his shoulder and set off down the smaller road which led into a winding glen. On the south side of the glen, massive buttresses of rock, rough and scarred, rose sheer from the edge of a small loch, totally circular, with pitch-brown waters and sandy shores. The buttresses climbed high and on both sides spread into cliffs and scree-filled gullies, so forming a massive wall which dominated the whole glen. Beyond the cliffs, the ground climbed in rounded shoulders and counter-facing crags. Green and brown and blackened with blue, the mountains rose and the thin line of the road held far away on the opposing side of the glen, high too and massive but less threatening in its rising. After a mile or so, the glen opened out into a strath where a chain of lochs, trembling in the light, stretched away into the distance. Here the road too broadened slightly, moved away from the mountainside and ran smoothly westwards to where the walls of the glen sank and the great flat headland began.

But it was to be quite some time before Murdo came clear of the glen. He walked along with that elongated, exaggerated stride, his hands plucking at the heavy growth on his chin, his eyes bright and peering, his face twitching from time to time as he took in his surroundings. Apart from the occasional sound from a sheep on the hillside above, Murdo heard only the gritty crunching of his boots on the road and the slight whistle of his breath.

A car came up from behind. He half-turned, hopefully, but the two men, tweed jackets and club ties, scarcely noticed him. He walked on, watching the corner of the falling sun reflected in the waters of the loch below him. Two more cars passed but they were both full of holidaymakers and were piled high with cases and belongings. After that, with the sun suddenly gone, a new kind of silence fell on the glen.

The last half-hour of the journey he made under cover of a strange light, neither night nor day, which lay across the northern landscape in a protracted twilight. It left the countryside visible yet without perspective so that Murdo felt his vision twisted and drunken. He steered blindly, following the telegraph poles and the dim slash of the road as it wound through a half-sensed world. He came to a collection of sleeping houses only to find it a complex of massive rocks. At another point he thought himself lost as the road ran down to an empty bay: but it turned and set off again inland. He found himself flanked by grey shields of water, heard the hollow chuckling of underground burns. The noise of wings, unidentified, marked brief points in the desolation across which he moved.

He stumbled on westwards, with the mountains' impenetrable walls now well behind and before him the great tongue of land that was bounded by the vast, dozing sea. He was just beginning to despair when, rounding a small rise, he saw the lights and faint shapes of a village standing, vaguely distant, before him. He stopped and blinked.

Murdo knew that the Mathesons' croft stood well outside Drienach. He looked around to see if there was any sign of a house on this side of the village. Nothing but half and whole darkness: no glimmer of habitation. He paused and looked back to see the village lights prickling, bright seeds in the warm night's womb.

When he was a hundred yards or so from the first houses, he stepped off the road and into the cover of a large rock.

At the near end of the village, a single, bright street lamp cast a bell of light on the roadway where a group of children were gathered. Outside the group, two boys circled lazily on bicycles.

When they came racing out into the dark, Murdo waited

till one had gone back and then called softly to the other.

'Here!'

The boy braked and skidded to a halt. Straddling the bicycle, he stared round, a silhouette of surprise and fright.

'Here, can you tell me where Bessie Matheson stays?'

'Bessie Matheson? Aye, she stays out at Camascoille. Over there.' The boy pointed out beyond the village.

'And what'll be the best way of getting there?'

'Well ... You go through the village and just keep following the road. When you come to Ruarach – a wee white house – you'll find a track away to the right. That's the way to the Mathesons.'

'Right.'

Murdo nodded and waited for the boy to go.

Crossing the road, Murdo stumbled slowly into the rough ground and began to make his way round the village. When he came to the back of the houses, he moved more quickly in the thin light thrown by the village street but in his haste, he tripped and jagged his hand on a loose strand of barbed wire. Wading across a slimy burn, he returned to the road and slipped away into the darkness, leaving the village behind him.

Now the full night was down. But the pale, reverberating light of the stars enabled Murdo to pick his way along the narrow road. Once he had passed over a small shoulder of land, the village fell away out of sight. But almost immediately, at some indeterminate distance, a bright light came into view, deeply embedded in the thick folds of the night. Murdo's tackety boots, heavy on the grit of the road, measured out his approach. Warily, he guided his steps on to the ridge of grass that ran down the middle so that he now moved with only a soft flurrying.

Gradually the light drew nearer. It was an outside light fixed high above the doorway of a small white house. Its brightness threw fat rolls of shadow beneath the eaves, made the walls glow and flooded across the layer of needles that lay beneath the cluster of dwarf pines close by the house. Within the quiltings of the darkness, this small pocket of light was full of stillness and warmth. By now, there was no trace of a wind and the crush of resin and heat hovered close to the ground. Without realizing it, Murdo had slowed his pace.

There was no sign of life inside the house. The door was open but because of a jutting lintel, nothing could be seen within. Yet Murdo found himself tiptoeing on the grass.

'Hello there.'

Murdo stopped dead. The immensely deep and soft voice which had issued forth from the doorway was followed by a small flash of light as the speaker lit his pipe. Murdo caught a glimpse of a thin face with two patches of pure white hair and a moustache.

'Hello.'

'It'll be Camascoille you're wanting.'

'Aye, that's right.'

There was a long pause while the man sucked determinedly at his pipe, concentrating so hard on the job of getting it properly lit that he appeared to have forgotten Murdo was there. Smoke rose in profusion, passed across the kernel of hard light above the door and was lost in the night. Murdo stood there foolishly, not sure if there was more to be said.

'It'll be a fine night for walking . . .'

The man came forward into the light. He was dressed in an old sweater and dirty trousers. He was very tall and thin but strongly built and looked younger than his white hair suggested. The skin of his face was shiny and drawn tight over his cheekbones. The bald part of his head was peeled and mottled pink. His eyes narrowed in the smoke from his pipe and then relaxed. The thick lips pursed

77

around the pipe's stem. For a moment, the lines of a smile appeared and then vanished. The eyes never blinked.

'. . . but you'll have come a long way though.'

'Aye, I have that, right enough. Is it far to Camascoille from here?'

There was another long pause before the man spoke again. His eyes had still not moved, Murdo's face twitched and contorted.

'What?' The man was staring at him. 'No . . . no . . . Just go up the road a wee way and you'll find a track off to the right. It's about a mile or so along there. You'll need to mind how you go, right enough, but you'll see the light from the house once you're over the burn.'

'Right. Thanks very much.'

The man's look was disconcerting. Murdo felt that he should be on his way. He knew that he would be better off not speaking to people more than he had to. He should just turn away and be gone. But without knowing exactly why, he stayed there, shuffling his feet about in the grass and looking up and down and around as he tried to break clear of the man's smiling gaze.

'Do you stay by yourself out here?' he asked quietly.

The man's eyes closed dreamily as if he were momentarily slipping away.

'Aye,' he said and his eyes opened again and now shone even brighter than before. 'Aye, there's just me and the dogs at Ruarach these days. My father's been gone these six years past . . . And will you be stopping long at Camascoille?'

'Och, I don't rightly know . . . No, I don't suppose I will.'

'Well, I'm sure you'll like it out here. It's quiet, mind you – but I dare say you could do with a bit of that.'

Murdo glanced suspiciously at the man and then looked down at the ground.

'Aye,' he said.

'And will Bessie be expecting you?'

'Well . . . I couldn't say . . . but . . .'

'Well now, you'll be Murdo,' interrupted the man.

Murdo swallowed slowly and blinked. He laughed nervously and then spoke as calmly as he could.

'And how did you know that then?'

The man drew on his pipe and smiled again. Murdo stood there with his mouth open in amazement. Suddenly, he was filled with a desire to tell the man everything, to confess what he had done. He longed for understanding and forgiveness. But instead he pulled himself together and said gruffly that he ought to be on his way.

The man nodded amicably and stood for a brief moment chewing at his pipe before he spoke.

'Cheerio then. I'll be seeing you again.'

He drew on his pipe, released the smoke and fanned it away from his face. A sullen look of anguish appeared in his eyes. Then, as if suddenly remembering himself, he smiled broadly and spoke again.

'My name's Hector.'

Murdo nodded and turned away into the darkness. As he left the road and went down the track to Camascoille, he glanced round and saw the man leaning back against the white wall, watching a blossom of smoke expanding above his head.

Five minutes later, Murdo passed over a small rushing burn and saw the light of the croft-house below him. For a moment he stopped, aware of his tiredness and the problems of confronting his sister. He breathed deeply and walked on.

At last he stood before the house. A dim light showed through the curtains of one window. The stars waited overhead. Nearby, a soft surf rolled constantly. Acheninver was locked far away in his memory. He bit at his lower lip and knocked on the door. For a moment there was no sound in the house; then the dull tread of steps and the door opened.

'Murdo!'

'Hello, Bessie.'

CHAPTER FIVE

For a moment brother and sister stood staring at each other in the doorway. It seemed to Murdo that Bessie had shrunk in the twelve years since he had last seen her. Her shoulders were rounded and she had a slight stoop: almost as if she had just been punched in the stomach. Her hair was quite grey and all her features had become soft and loose as the skin of her face had lost its resilience. As she stood in the doorway her jaw trembled, her lips pressed together and her eyes became glossy. Murdo felt ashamed of himself.

'Well, you'd best come in.' Bessie spoke with that gentle but matter-of-fact voice that Murdo remembered from his youth. 'But heavens, man, what have you gone and done to yourself? You're covered in mud and, oh, look at your hand!'

Murdo looked down and saw that his hand was netted with blood from where he had torn it on the barbed wire.

He walked in and Bessie shut the door. As it closed behind him and the outside world was barred, Murdo drew in his breath and caught the homely smells of his sister's house. The mustiness of old clothes, dog, paraffin and tobacco was crossed and tangled with yeast and flour and crust and the comforting sour-edged smell of warm bodies. The small hallway was lit by a paraffin lamp whose tent of light encased the two of them. Murdo pressed his hands to his eyes.

Bessie took him into the kitchen. Mary Matheson was sitting at the table smoking a cigarette, her mass of hair illuminated by the light of the lamp which burned on the shelf behind her. She said hello and smiled.

In the scullery Murdo soaped his face and hands. He looked up and caught sight of the stranger staring at him out of the mirror with red-rimmed eyes in a face of soap and stubble. The sound of plates and quiet conversation drifted to him as he stood there in the lamplight. His hands were trembling.

He tried to reassure himself. He had got away from Acheninver and had arrived safely in his new life. Still he stared at himself. The object had been achieved. He blinked. But the achievement brought him neither pleasure nor relief; only new fear. Everybody, even Bessie, his own sister, would be waiting to see what he was going to do. The arrival at Camascoille was no home-coming. He was just a visitor in these people's lives. It must only be a matter of time before he would be moving on.

Murdo dropped his hands to the edge of the basin and stared down into the water.

When he returned to the kitchen, it was a relief to him to be able to busy himself with the eggs and wedges of newly baked bread that Bessie set before him. He ate without pausing, fearing that a moment's hesitation would bring questions. But Bessie saw how things were and let him be, talking instead to Mary about Camas-coille. Mary did not say very much but was watching Murdo over her cup of tea. Soon after he had finished eating, she said that she was tired and would be away to her bed. She left them and a while later, movements were heard in the room above.

Bessie and Murdo sat without talking as if listening to Mary overhead. They sipped at their tea, both looking down at the table. Soon there was silence upstairs. Murdo fiddled with a box of matches. Bessie got up to get him some more tea and then sat down again. The paraffin lamp flickered once, twice. They both looked up at it.

Shadows and smells wallowed in the outer parts of the room.

'Murdo, in heaven's name, what's happened with you and Margaret?'

And so the question was finally asked. Murdo looked surprised for a moment, not understanding how Bessie could know what had happened. But when she explained that the minister had written, he began to tell her his story. He told her how things had not been so good between him and Margaret for a long while, how he could no longer stay with her now that Flora was gone and that he had just left home. Bessie prompted him as he stumbled over his words.

'So you're not thinking of going back?'

'No. That I won't do.'

'So what are you going to do?'

'Well . . . I don't exactly know, right enough. I was thinking that if I could stop here a wee while . . .'

'Aye. You know well enough that you can. But I don't know how Alec and Mary will take it. You see, with the three of us and young Dougie, we're a bit short of space.'

'Aye, Bessie. Aye, I know that but . . .'

'You know that if it were only me, you could stop as long as you had a mind to.'

'Now don't you worry yourself, Bessie. I'll just stop a day or two while I make my plans and then I'll be away and nobody'll be bothered.'

'And what'll you do, Murdo? There's no much work around these parts at the moment.'

'No? Ach well, I'll find myself something. Don't you go worrying about that . . .'

For a long time they sat talking quietly. Bessie opened the window to let in some air and so the sound of the moving sea was there and breaking gently about them. A while later, there was the noise of the front door closing.

'That'll be Alec.'

But Murdo seemed not to hear Bessie speak. He only looked up when the kitchen door opened and the thickset man came in and stood in the doorway, breathing heavily.

'Alec, this is my brother Murdo.'

'Hello.'

Alec's greeting could not have been colder. He closed the door behind him and slumped into an armchair with his back to Bessie and Murdo.

'Will you take a cup of tea, Alec?'

'No thanks, Bessie. Where's Mary?'

'Oh she was away to her bed a while ago. She said she was tired.'

'She likes her sleep, my woman does. Are you staying the night?' Alec's voice was muffled with drink. He had kicked the chair round and was looking at Murdo.

'Aye,' said Murdo.

'And where'll you be thinking of sleeping then?'

'Alec! That's no way to be speaking. You need to mind your tongue when you've been out. We'll make up a bed for him in here.'

Alec stared at his feet. Bessie and Murdo went on talking about Acheninver, ignoring Alec who never moved, though his eyes watched them from the darkness of the chair. After a few minutes he got up and left the room.

'Ach, take no notice of him, Murdo. He doesn't mean any harm. It's just the drink in him talking . . . Come on now, we'll make you a bed. You'll be wanting your sleep, I'm thinking.'

When Bessie had gone off to bed and a heavy stillness had settled on the house, Murdo sat at the table a while longer. He gazed through the open window at the sound of the sea while the wedge of the lamp's buttery flame stood calm and erect above him.

There was no self-pity in the look on his face for his was

a suffering of brute pain, which brought him only lethargy and numbness. He gazed intently, hypnotized by the nothingness. All he felt was a dull awareness that he must keep going; for it was ahead that safety and the end lay waiting for him. Even now, in his despondency, Murdo did not lose his conviction that everything would turn out well in the end. He did not know how or when; indeed the fifty-eight years of his life had given him little on which to base such a belief. Happiness had always been just beyond his reach; yet he knew that it was there. This trust was the one untouchable thing in Murdo Munro's mind.

He wrinkled up his face and rubbed the end of his nose with the palm of his hand. He glanced over at his bed – some blankets and an old mattress laid in the corner – and getting up from the table, began to undress. Blowing out the lamp, he slipped into bed and lay staring upwards, thinking of his nights on Eilean na Rainich. Then he turned on his side and immediately fell asleep.

He slept in a deep, dreamless trench of sleep, knowing nothing of the changing night, unaware of the darkness beginning to drain away, leaving the mountain ridges backed by a pale light. And even when the sun finally managed to haul itself into view; even when the still sea, breathing in a shallow swell, was touched by the light far out from the land, even then, with all the small crackings and muted cries of a waking world, Murdo did not stir. It was only an hour or so later that he awoke with a start and twisted round to look at the figure of the small boy standing in the doorway.

'Who are you?' the boy asked in amazement.

Murdo's head fell back on the pillow as his dozing mind tried to think who he was in the boy's eyes.

'I'm . . . I'm Murdo, Bessie's brother.'

'Oh . . . Can I come in? I'm wanting my breakfast and the others'll not be up for a while yet.'

'Aye, aye. Come in. Don't mind me . . . What time is it?'

'Well, I don't rightly know. But it'll be near on half-past six I should think.'

But Murdo was already asleep again. When he next woke, the boy was gone. He got up and went out. As he opened the door he felt the bright-hot hand of the sun seize him across the face.

The croft-house was set in a small dip through a single gap in whose rim the sea was to be seen. Coarse deer-grass covered the ground and this was quite unbroken except for the clawed marks of the track.

Up above, the sky showed clear but for a few strips of cloud and the great power of the sun.

Just grass and sea and sky.

Even the house itself, its four windows placed symmetrically around the doorway, reflected this simplicity.

Murdo looked up at the sun and then shook his head to rid himself of the light, like a dog coming out of the water. He heard Bessie call to him, her voice sounding soft and cool in the early morning heat. When he returned to the kitchen, Alec was already down and eating his breakfast. He nodded to Murdo, his unshaven jaw chewing methodically, his eyes staring and cold. Murdo made some remark about the weather but Alec just continued to stare and made no answer.

And so it was to be between Murdo and Alec. In the days that followed, each time that Murdo offered to help, the younger man turned him down. Bessie stood by helplessly, anxious to keep the peace in the house.

To begin with, Mary was friendly enough. She smiled at Murdo and occasionally talked to him, but this merely served to drive Alec deeper into his silence. And though she tried to soften his attitude, he was implacable.

It was perhaps that Alec himself had too often been involved with the police, both in Drienach and earlier in

86

Glasgow, for him to be pleased at housing a man who was in trouble with them. For Bessie had told him that something had happened in Acheninver, that Murdo could not go back for the moment. Of course, neither of them knew precisely what Murdo had done, but Alec was suspicious. Out of deference to Bessie, he put up with Murdo's presence; but nothing could persuade him to accept the man. And after a while Mary tired of trying to reconcile him to Murdo and saw that there would be no peace while Murdo remained. There was not much joy at Camascoille when they all gathered for their tea in the early evening.

But it was young Dougie who alleviated Murdo's position at Camascoille. When he saw Murdo sitting around with nothing to do, he came up and asked if he would like to come and see the otter. He asked with such seriousness, such politeness, his dark eyes wide open in question, that Murdo laughed and said that indeed he would. Dougie's offer, spoken with such a strange mixture of reticence and childish bluntness, had totally disarmed him.

Of course, the otter failed to appear but Dougie quickly forgot his disappointment and took Murdo to see the place where he had found the mergansers nesting earlier in the year. On the way back, they crossed the burn and Dougie pointed out the remains of a dam he had built in the spring. Murdo, caught up by the boy's enthusiasm, said that they ought to repair it and, rolling up his sleeves, began to collect rocks and heathers.

By the time they had completed the dam, they were both covered in mud. Murdo stood there, wiping his forehead with his forearm while Dougie went around trying the strength of their work.

The building of the dam gained Murdo an unshakeable friend. Seemingly oblivious to the tension between his father and Murdo, Dougie unwittingly did much to maintain a balance of humour in the household. Murdo, who had insisted on making his bed in the hay-loft in the byre, was now woken every morning by the boy's calling.

'Hey, Murdo! Murdo! Are you coming down? It's another great day.'

'Aye, Dougie. Just you away to your breakfast and I'll be with you in a minute.'

One morning, Murdo was woken as usual by Dougie's voice.

'Hey, Murdo! Hector's here to see you.'

'Hector? Who's Hector?'

'Hector! Hector Ruarach, you know, the shepherd who stays down at the road-end.'

'Oh aye. Is it me he's wanting?'

'Aye. So he says.'

Murdo struggled into his boots and dropped down from the loft. Dougie had disappeared. Murdo came out of the byre and looked around. It was still early. The sun was white and low in the sky, sending long lights and shadows across the land. Hector was leaning against the wheel of the old tractor, paring his nails with a penknife. Facing into the sun, his mottled forehead and white wings of hair were full of light. He looked up and saw Murdo and a broad, sleepy smile awoke on his face.

'Hello, Murdo. And how are you keeping?'

'Oh, I can't complain . . .'

There was a wary pause between the two men. Hector's shadow, enormously long, was momentarily distorted as a sheep passed through it.

'Another good day, I'd say,' ventured Murdo.

'Aye, it will be, right enough . . . Are they keeping you busy here, eh?'

'Aye . . . no . . . well, you know how it is – a bit here, a bit there. There's always something to be done and I'm not one to be sitting around idle . . . But we could be doing with a bit of wind. It's hellish hot.'

'Aye, it is so . . .' Hector pauses and looks out to sea. Then he turns back and speaks again but more slowly. 'Murdo . . . I just came across to say that if you're ever wanting away in a hurry, perhaps I can help you.'

'Me? How do you mean? Why should I be wanting away in a hurry?' Murdo's voice sounds aggresive. But Hector takes no notice.

'Och well, you never know. I just thought I'd tell you. I'd best be on my way.'

And his great lithe form springs upright from the tractor wheel.

'Here now, wait a minute, Hector . . .' Hector turns and looks down at Murdo. Murdo realizes just how tall the man is. 'Has somebody been talking to you?'

'No, no! And who would be doing that anyway?'

'Och, I don't know. Somebody here perhaps.' Murdo gestures towards the croft-house.

'No, I've no heard anything at all. No, I just had the feeling that if you were wanting away, you'd not be knowing any of the folk in these parts. But just you forget what I said. No harm meant. Anyway, you'll always know where to find me.'

And with a smile, he turns and walks away and on to the track towards Ruarach.

Murdo watched him go. He stood for a while, kicking at a loose rock with his heavy boot. Then he went in to get his breakfast. When the others had gone and Murdo was alone with Bessie, he asked her about Hector.

'Hector? Well, there are people around here who laugh at him and say he's a wee bit simple; but they don't know him as I do. He's a good man. He was one of the first to come and lend a hand after Duncan died. He used to be a shepherd on an estate way out on the other side of Drienach. His father had worked there too and Hector took over from him after the war. But the estate got into some money trouble and eventually it was sold and broken up. And now it's hard to say what the man lives on. He works here and there, right enough, but he hasn't got much . . . But when did you see him?'

'Well, I met him on the way out here, the night I arrived. And then I saw him just now when he was over.'

'When? Today? I didn't know he'd been here. I haven't seen him for a couple of weeks . . . What a man! He might have come in and said hello to me. I'd have given him a bite to eat.'

Murdo falls silent for a moment, puzzled.

'Is he a friend of Alec's?'

'No, I wouldn't say that. Alec's got no time for him. Says he's daft . . . Ach, you know how Alec can be.'

'And what makes people say he's simple?'

'Well, it's true that Hector says some queer things, things that can worry folk. But I don't think it's that so much. I think it's more the kind of life he leads. He's always alone and sometimes in the summer he goes away to the hills with his dog and nobody sets eyes on him for a week or two. Well, why not? If that's what the man likes, there's no harm in it. But nowadays there's a lot of folk just interested in their comforts who think it queer if a man does differently and prefers the old kind of life . . .'

After Murdo had been at Camascoille for nearly a week, Alec relented and gave him a few odd jobs to do. It was not out of any change of heart but more because he himself was pressed by the amount of work to be done. A large part of the Mathesons' income in the summer months came from Alec's fishing for lobsters and while he was out at sea there were things on the croft which had to go neglected. As Murdo was obviously going to stay a while longer, it seemed to Alec that he might as well make himself useful. The door to the byre needed repairing, some slates on the croft-house roof were loose, there was some new ground to be dug. Murdo set himself to work on the door to the byre, as always with Dougie's help, and although Alec never actually gave him a word of thanks, the precedent was set. Now, at least, there was less need for Murdo to go.

One day, Murdo and Dougie were out repairing a fence. The sun stood high above them. There was no wind and the flies and clegs were everywhere. After an hour or two of working in the heat, they took a break and sat down in a patch of heathers. Murdo picked up the splinter of a stob and started to shape it with his knife into the figure of a man.

'Is that going to be a man or a woman, Murdo?'

'I don't rightly know yet. What'll you have?'

'Make it an old woman. All skinny and bent.'

Murdo laughed.

'Would you not rather have a young one, a bonny one?'

'Ach, no! What would I be wanting her for . . .? Do you have a woman, Murdo?'

'Well . . . aye in a manner of speaking. That's to say, I used to.'

'How do you mean? Where's she now?'

'She's back at home . . . down south.'

'Oh . . . but won't you get a rowing if you stay away? That's what happens to my dad when he doesn't come home.'

Murdo smiled grimly.

'Well, you see, I've been away that long now that I'd be best not going back at all.'

This seemed to puzzle Dougie and he was silent for a moment or two before he spoke again.

'Have you got a mum and a dad?'

'No, they're long gone.'

'So who've you got then?'

'How do you mean, who have I got?'

'Well, everybody's got somebody, haven't they?'

'Aye . . . well, I suppose they have. Well . . . I've got Bessie.'

'Aye, but she's only your sister. You can't count her.'

'Right, well if I can't count her, I'll have to have a wee think . . .'

Murdo whittles away at the wood. Who had he got apart from Bessie?

'Well, I've got you, Dougie.'

'Aye, you've got me!' The boy sounded jubilant at the idea. 'So if you've got me and nobody else, you'll not need to be going away, will you now?'

'Why would I be thinking of going away?'

Dougie's face darkened and he looked down.

'Well . . . I heard my dad telling my mum that you'd need to be going soon – very soon. But you'll not, will you?'

Murdo stopped cutting at the wood. The sunlight seemed black, the sea glaring. Dougie's voice was distant.

'Murdo!'

Murdo looked at the boy and saw his eyes, wide and full of fright. He smiled and got to his feet.

'Come on now, we'll need to finish this fencing.'

All the rest of that day, Murdo's mind kept returning to what the boy had said. Even if he was working and earning his keep, there was little point in him staying at Camascoille if Alec, and perhaps Mary too, wanted rid of him. For the past few days he had not given the prospect of leaving much thought; but now he tried once again to decide what he would do if he left Camascoille. He would need to have some definite plan to tell Bessie, for she would not let him go otherwise. And he had best slip away without telling Dougie . . .

That afternoon he worked sullen and angry. Dougie sensed it and went carefully, treading in fear of this brooding in the man which he did not understand. Murdo, seeing how nervous the boy was, only cursed himself the more. To rid himself of his bile, he thrust himself into his work. He handled the coiling barbed wire with a complete contempt for his own safety, feeling the relief of punishment as he jagged and ripped his hands on it.

Late in the afternoon, with the work done, they walked home in silence, Dougie not knowing how to talk to Murdo, Murdo bitter with shame at his own anger. Back at home, while Bessie dressed a cut on Murdo's neck, the boy slipped away and, after walking out of sight of the house, he slumped down on a rock and burst into tears.

That night, high up in the roof of the byre, Murdo lay sleeplessly in the darkness. In the last few days, the weather had changed. For the past three weeks and more, it had been hot and cloudless and then gradually the sky had begun to thicken, the colours darkening each day and the air becoming damp and heavy. By that evening, everybody had started to complain of the closeness and even with all the windows open there was little relief. Dougie, hours after he had gone to bed, reappeared in the kitchen, saying that he could not sleep.

The door of the byre was wide open yet even so the heat was oppressive. Through the open doorway, the moonlight cast a fish-tail of coolness across the floor. The nighttime silence was heavy as if the whole sky above were alive with trapped energy. The smells of the byre seemed putrid and cloying.

He turned from side to side, screwing up his face at the heat prickling all over his body and then, unable to bear it any longer, he got up and sprang down from the loft.

Outside the byre, Murdo breathed deeply and looked around. The whole bowl of land in which the croft-house stood was coated with the wash of the moon. Far across the sky, the moon itself, now in its third quarter, was wedged between two banks of cloud that had built up in the early hours of the night. Only rarely did the faint edge of a wind brush in off the sea. Otherwise the ground stood motionless in the moonlight, giving off its smells of peat and heathers and grass that joined with those from around the byre – the hay, the dung, the diesel, the rank oiliness of fleece and hide, the drying dust beneath a tap. Over on his left, the pallid face of the croft-house stared into the moonlight.

Murdo waited in the hope of a breath of wind; when none came, he wandered away from the buildings, following a sheep-track up to the western edge of the hollow. From here he could see the flat headland nosing out another three miles into the ocean waters. Neither road nor track; neither croft nor building of any kind; nothing but the deer-grass and peat and rock, nothing but moss and uncounted bog with loch and lochan the vague and scattered landmarks. But for all its mass, this piece of land was as nothing among the fields of the sea, its pools and patterns of current and tide. In the sickly, sweet airs of that August night even the sound of the light surf was muffled. From by the blackthorn bushes that grew behind the byre, a nightjar churred with its deep, unnatural trilling.

When Murdo turned back towards the byre, he thought he saw the figure of a man just below the skyline about a quarter of a mile away to the south. But when he looked again and saw nothing, he shrugged and continued on his way home.

The next morning the sun came up through a thick haze that blocked out the lower part of the sky. By ten o'clock, everybody was weighed down by the heat.

Murdo was up on the roof of the house, refixing a line of slates. Straddled high on the ridge, he worked quickly, wanting to finish the job before the full heat of the day was on them. But his head drooped and his arms seemed weak and ineffectual as he felt himself being caught between the heat of the sun's rays and the scorching surface of the slates. From time to time he stopped and stretched his aching back; and looking out to sea, saw Alec's boat creeping back down the coast from the point. Then, with a quick glance towards the sun, he would go back to his work. As he removed the old, heavy slates, he piled them up neatly by the chimney.

When Dougie came out from helping Bessie in the kitchen, he wanted to come up on the roof and give Murdo a hand. But Murdo told him it was too dangerous and that, besides, there was no room for the two of them. So Dougie just sat down disconsolately on the grass.

The sun grew steadily hotter.

'Hey Dougie!'

Alec's rough voice sounded up from the path to the shore.

'What?'

Murdo turned round. And as he did so, his elbow caught the edge of a pile of slates. He saw them go and made a desperate grab for them. But five or six of them had gone and were clattering down the steep pitch of the roof.

'Dougie!' Murdo's yell was sharp with fear.

The boy, standing close by the house, turned round. Squinting up into the light, he saw nothing but glare and shape; heard only the rattling sound above him. The first of the heavy plates shot over Dougie's shoulder and thudded into the ground. He started to duck but was not quick enough and the next one struck him a glancing blow on the head. He crumpled over on to the grass. In the following silence, a yowe bleated gutturally.

Murdo was scrambling down the ladder that lay hooked over the ridge of the roof. When he got to the gutter, he sprang out into space. He crashed to the ground and went sprawling but jumped up and ran to the boy's side. Dougie was moving slightly but blood oozed thickly down the side of his head.

'You bloody fool! What have you done to him?'

Alec came up behind Murdo and his powerful hand gripped his shoulder. With an almost effortless gesture, he pitched Murdo aside and bent down over his son.

As Murdo picked himself up, Dougie moved again and let out a moan of pain.

'Is he all right?'

'How do I know?' Alec's voice was only just controlled.

'Dougie boy, are you all right?' Murdo asked gently.

Alec, still squatting, swung round on Murdo, his eyes starting, his mouth twisted.

'Will you get away from the boy or I'll break your bloody head open!'

Murdo stepped back and saw Bessie hurrying round the corner.

'What happened?'

'I . . . Dougie's hurt.'

'Oh Lord, what've you done?'

Alec carried Dougie into the sitting room and laid him down. While Bessie began to sponge the boy's head, Alec said he would be away for the doctor. With an angry glance at Murdo, he slammed the door and was gone.

Dougie lay, white-faced and silent.

'Oh . . . my head!'

'There, there . . . You took a nasty knock. But you just lie still now and the doctor'll soon be here to see to you.'

Bessie stood up and the boy's eyes turned to see Murdo standing by the window.

'How do you feel, Dougie?'

'Oh . . . my head hurts something terrible. What happened? There was this noise.'

'Aye, it was the slates. Now just you lie still and you'll be fine.'

Dougie attempted a smile and looked slowly about him.

Fifty minutes later, the doctor's car came bumping down the track. Murdo slipped away. From beside the burn he watched the doctor and the others go into the house.

The little water there was in the burn bubbled its way downhill with an irritating monotony. A dipper, perched on a rock upstream, bobbed up and down. Murdo stared glumly at the bird. But the bird, neat in its white bib, just bobbed and bobbed and stared back. Murdo looked away and immediately it flew off upstream.

Sitting there in the heat, Murdo saw himself turning, the flash of sun, the half-seen stack of slates, the desperate lunge, the top of the boy's head beneath the gutter, with the clattering and his cry that, even now, came again and again like a gunshot in the mountains.

The noonday sun was now only the heart of the great white light that filled the sky for the heat itself seemed to emanate from all around. It rose up from the earth, it hung in flanking walls, it lay waiting in the dips and gullets of the rocks. Looking out from the coast, it seemed to have laid its force on the waters too, for the further part of the sea was invisible under the same white haze that hovered in the sky.

Until late in the afternoon, Murdo managed to keep out of the way. He learnt from Bessie that Dougie had been given a few stitches but that he was going to be all right, though he must stay in bed for a day or two. Anxious to remove the reminder of the accident, Murdo went up on the roof again and finished replacing the slates. When this was done, he put away the ladders and went down to the shore.

It was only when he thought that they would have finished their tea that he came back. Seeing Bessie and Mary out with the hens beyond the house and reckoning that Alec would be on his way in to the hotel in Drienach, Murdo came round the side of the house and quietly walked in. Opening the kitchen door, he found himself face to face with Alec who was sitting smoking at the table.

'Oh . . . I was just thinking I'd get myself a bite to eat.'

Alec nodded and looked away.

'How's Dougie doing?'

'He'll be all right.'

A silence.

'Look, Alec – I'm sorry about what . . .'

'Don't waste your breath, man. I'm no interested to hear what you've got to say. So when'll you be thinking of leaving then?'

'How do you mean?'

'Well, you came here to visit Bessie, did you no? And you've done that.'

'Well, I'm not quite sure yet but . . .'

'But you'll know soon, won't you?'

'Aye . . . I should think so,' Murdo answered quietly.

He picked up his piece and walked out. Leaving the house, he met Bessie and Mary on their way back. Mary looked away and walked past him.

'Look, Bessie, seeing how things are, I'm thinking I'd best be on my way.'

There was a tired look in Bessie's eyes.

'But where'll you go, Murdo?'

'Well I've been thinking. Perhaps it would be best if I went back to Acheninver and tried to sort things out . . .'

'Aye, Murdo,' answered Bessie, looking pleased, 'that's what I've been thinking all along. You know, you're not so young any more. You can't just throw away your life like that. If you can just try and talk to Margaret . . . or go and see the minister as he asks, I'm sure it'll all . . .'

Bessie went on with her ideas. With her woman's concern for security, she told him that surely some kind of a home was always better than none. But Murdo was not listening. It was not only that he did not agree with Bessie; it was also because he had no intention of going back to Acheninver and had only told her so in the hope of placating her.

But as he left her and walked away past the byre, munching his piece, he realized that if he was not going back to Acheninver, he must have somewhere else to go: for after the happenings of the day, he knew that he now had to leave Camascoille. Well, he could always try one or two of the ports to the south and if there were no work there, he would go across to the East Coast . . .

As the sun started to come down into the indistinct wash above the horizon, the heat began to lessen. But with this came the midges. They collected in dense columns, twisting and swirling like smoke above the bushes and brackens. They rose up from under Murdo's feet as he walked. They arrived, uncounted, from nowhere to form new clouds and swarms. And as Murdo passed into their midst, they fell upon him in their masses.

And then, suddenly, so unexpectedly that Murdo literally blinked in surprise, a little wind turned in off the sea. Once, twice, it stroked at him, cool and light, and the midges were gone. He scratched at his stinging head and passed on along the coast.

He walked with no intent, yet all the same moved quickly, finding the rhythm a balm to his turbulent mind. Further and further he walked, at one moment following the shore, at another cutting across the back of a promontory to weave in among the lochans with their pink-stemmed reeds and burnished bright waters. And again now, his pace had quickened as if he were racing against something, as if he were driven by desire for what lay before him. Onwards he went, stamping and sliding over the moss and peat, running down to leap burns and clefts, scrambling up again and heading off ever westwards. And then, with a final bound, he sprang down on to a slab of rock and stopped.

He had come to the farthest edge of the land and stood alone, cut off from the distant world. The rock on which he was poised jutted out over the deep, whispering waters that lay a hundred and twenty feet below him. Black, glistening rocks prickled through the salt foam. A handful of fulmars dived and peeled against the rock-face where fern and grass sprouted from ledge and crevice.

He looked up and his complete vision was filled by the sight of the sea. Everything on the water was of metal and blood and fire. And even above the horizon, the sky was thick with smoke and flames. On three sides of him, the light surf hushed and rustled ceaselessly.

Murdo looked down again. The swell bent and rolled, bent and rolled. As he watched, he found himself nodding and beginning to sway gently with the movement of the waters. An irresistible sleepiness stunned his limbs.

He was three miles across rough ground from the nearest house. The sea before him was empty. The rock on which he stood overhung the cliff. If he stepped forwards . . . If he stepped forwards, he would touch nothing.

The swell bent and rolled.

He stood there, staring down at the sea, for a quarter of an hour. The light of the setting sun rose off the water and fired him into a deep, glowing colour, his starting eyes dazzled and shiny. There was a look of intense concern, of agitation almost, on his beaten face. Fulmars passed close below him unnoticed. A small school of porpoises, only a hundred and fifty yards off the point, went unseen as they arched through the surface of the sea.

When the moment had passed, his eyes flickered and he frowned. He cast one wide look over the sea and then started back across the land. As he went, he saw far beyond the croft of Camascoille, far beyond a deep-bitten bay in the coast, the confusion of mountains rising from the lowlands of rock.

Arriving back at Camascoille in the twilight, he went straight to his bed in the loft and, unaware of the heat, fell asleep.

CHAPTER SIX

As if struck sharply on the back of the head, Murdo jolted forward out of his sleep. The dream was already gone: only the urgent tapping of his heart stayed as a waking reminder of the horror. He rolled on to his back, breathed in deeply and expelled the breath upwards into the vaulting of the rafters. Above him sounded the scratching of birds' feet on the roof. The liquid, sorrowing call of curlews came up from the direction of the shore. He turned his head and saw a collie appear snuffling at the byre door. The dog stopped to look up at the man and then trotted away.

Murdo came down from the loft and paused in the doorway. As he expected, there was the sound of conversation, an indistinct murmuring suspended in the morning sunlight. He walked slowly across to the croft-house and peered round the corner. He caught a quick glimpse of Hector's back and the seemingly diminutive form of Bessie standing beyond him. Drawing back out of sight, he stood pinned by the sun against the whitewashed gable-end of the building and tried to hear what they were saying. The hollow resonance of Hector's voice came to him clearly.

'Well, where's he now?'

Bessie's reply was soft and indistinct.

'But why should the police come out here, Bessie? Sergeant MacDonald knows well enough that you're not to blame for what he's done . . .'

Again Bessie replied.

'Oh aye . . . I see what you mean,' Hector said slowly.

Murdo waited but Hector left the subject and started talking of a coming sheep sale. Turning away towards the byre, Murdo's jaw hung loose as his mind swelled in panic.

In the three weeks since he had fled from Acheninver, he had lived with an undercurrent of fear running deeply in his mind. Having burnt his house and deserted his woman, he had woken each morning with the expectation of some retribution. And with each day passing without news from the south, he had found himself being slowly unnerved.

The oppressiveness of this fear had been building up through the silence of these days of long heat, had swelled almost ungauged in the chaos of his mind so that when he heard the mention of the police, the underlying thoughts had risen up and come thundering down across his consciousness in a surf of panic.

And now, hurrying back to the byre, he was intent only on getting away from Camascoille as fast as he could. He ripped the corner off a heavy paper bag containing hen food and rummaging in his pockets for the stub of a pencil, hastily wrote Bessie a note.

Dear Bessie –
Have taken some food for journy.
Am leaving £1 for same. Also £1 please
by Dougie something. Am very sorry.
Cheerio now.
Murdo

Then shouldering his coat and bag, he crept out of the byre. Hector had gone and Bessie was over with her hens. He went to the house and keeked in at the kitchen window. Nobody. Furtively he came round the side of the house and keeping an eye on Bessie, slipped in at the front door.

Once in the kitchen, he crammed his bag with oddments of food from the larder and stuffed a slice of cheese into his mouth. With its crumblings falling from his lips, he laid the message and two pound notes on the table and was just turning to go when he heard someone at the front door. He moved quickly round the table and with a heave and a grunt pulled himself through the open window and on to the grass outside. Without even looking over his shoulder, he ran for the path that led down to the shore.

And a moment later, Camascoille had passed out of his life.

Once out of sight of the house, he stopped to regain his breath. His heart knocked insistently at his ribs. The police would not be long in coming out from Drienach. He looked up and saw the thick, heat-riven bands of cloud and sky. He would need to get well clear of the croft. Beside him the sea lay trapped by the windless heat. Under the bright light, the surface was like a heavy layer of oil covering the vague shape of a swell. He felt himself cornered. Effortlessly, the surface gave before the soft rising of the water and then fell back to its former flatness, the undulation moving onwards to escape in a gentle puff of foam at the shore. He seemed unable to move. Which way should he turn? Gulls and terns, looking indolent in the early morning heat, floated on the offshore waters. Occasionally, one of them would rise laboriously into the air and give a few lazy flaps of its wings before gliding down and subsiding again. An oystercatcher and three black-headed gulls stood motionless on a tangle-covered rock.

For a brief moment, his head sagged. Then he looked up and started to walk along the coast towards the east.

He quickly settled into his stride. To avoid the rocks and tangle, he kept on the ground just above the shore, yet always below the skyline from where he could have been seen from Drienach. In spite of his fast pace, his progress was slow for the ground was cut by numerous burns and the deep drainings of peat-hags. In and out of the small bays and creeks he moved, twisting on with the contortions of the ground; until suddenly he came round a sharp point and saw far out before him the lower edge of the hills that lined the mainland beyond the promontory.

With these hills in sight, Murdo's spirits rose. If he could only get off the promontory he would have room to move. He walked quickly but with a restraint, a stiffness in his movements; while his eyes went endlessly backwards and forwards across the ground before him. Judging that he was by now well past Drienach, he moved up from the shore and so on to flatter ground. He saw the road, marked by telegraph poles, only a short way off, a causeway across the acres of flatness and floating peat. It ran out from Drienach, closed with the coast for a mile or so and then bent its way back among the lochs before disappearing into the glen beyond. Coming up on to the tarmac, it seemed strange to him that he had first walked this road only such a short time before.

Once or twice he heard the distant drone of an approaching car and slipped off the road to lie like a beast in a covert of the ground till it had passed away out of sight. After the last of these had disappeared, an intense silence spread across the plain and Murdo gradually fell into a hazy sense of unreality. The fierce, dusty heat of the sky, the toneless sound of the humming in the wires and the wavering strip of tarmac pulling away before him – all combined to draw him downwards into a waking sleep in which the only dimension was the rhythm of his tackety boots on the grit at the road's edge.

He stopped and splashed his face with water from a nearby pool; he rubbed at his eyes and shook his head. But each time, after only a few minutes of walking, the soft fingers of sleep closed gently about him so that he fell back into a state of mindlessness in which he continued to walk without knowing either how or why he did so. It was only when a voice at his shoulder greeted him and a bicyclist passed that he finally woke from his trance.

As he stood and watched the bicyclist's hunched form grow smaller in the distance, Murdo realized that he had had enough of this creeping and hiding. There was shame in it and he longed to be away into the hills and out of sight of the people and places that reminded him of his failure.

At the point where the promontory's northern shore joined that of the mainland proper, the ground rose away from the flatness in a series of stark hills, encrustations of knobbled rock where patches of peat and grass clung as best they could. Their low heights came almost to the sea before dropping away in ramps and bare crags to form a coastline rough with complexes of chasms and dark cleavings. No croft, no fank, no dry-stone wall, no anchored boat, no sign whatever of habitation but mile upon mile of sunlit wilderness.

Yet for all these forbidding qualities, it was with relief and anticipation that Murdo stepped off the road and began to climb slowly up the slope of the hills. The weeks of hot weather had done little or nothing to dry out the land. Here and there, he came upon patches of black peat on which the sun had formed a crust; though beneath the cracks and wrinkles of the surface on which white strands of the winter grasses lay fixed, the mud was soft and deep.

He scrambled upwards, his boots rasping on the rock and sinking into the quaking bogs and water-borne grasses. His way was threaded with the sound of water, the gurgling of an underground burn, the splash and trickle from a hanging moss bed, the gush and light pounding from a rocky gut. With the sun now overhead and the heat overpowering on the bare hillside, these liquid, hidden noises were things of mystery.

He stopped and wiped his forehead. There was a dull. buzzing in his head; his eyes stung from the sweat. He swallowed, licked his lips and looked up at the hill. A great fist of gritty rock stood punched up into the sky several hundred feet above him. He turned and sat down.

Already far below him, the road was only a grey vein in the tongue of the land. The village, away on his right, was a smudge on the ground, an insignificant outpost; while beyond, the croft-house at Camascoille stood like a white mote, a single gull locked in the haze. The mass of pools and lochans lay under the light, sparkling, wriggling, a shoal of flounders. Here and there, the shelving of a dun-coloured beach showed up the peatiness of their waters.

As Murdo started to eat his lunch, he gazed down at a piece of yellow moss between his feet and wondered where he should go. And as he thought on this, so too, there rose in him a great brooding sensation of his solitude. It was not so much the solitude of the present moment but more the realization that, a mere year or so before his sixtieth birthday, he found himself with all the links to the life he knew severed and a future hard to imagine. Indeed, was it possible for a man like him to construct a whole new existence, he wondered. To lose his job and find another one – aye. To lose his woman and find another one – well, perhaps. But he had lost his job, his woman, his house, had alienated himself from his sister and was in trouble with the police . . . It was not even as if he could any longer be among friends for the few he had were in Acheninver. And moodily he thought of Flora and the shame he had brought upon her. And even to wee Dougie, he had been a disappointment, a friend vanishing into the night without a goodbye.

He had had his life, he had had his chance. If he were to vanish now, who would feel the loss? But perhaps that was the wrong way to think . . . He tried to imagine what he himself wanted from the world; but no, nothing came to mind. So it seemed to him that whichever way he looked at it, there was little point. He tore at a piece of bread and tossed the crust aside.

And yet, even with the blankness of despair folding about him, even with the image of a lonely old age before him, there remained a small, still flame burning untouched far down in some recess of his soul. And it was perhaps a slight shimmering of this that he felt as a fierce smile opened briefly on his face. He struck his thigh with his fist and got to his feet. Swinging his bag over his shoulder, he turned and saw there was still a good way to climb.

Passing over the top of a rise, he came out above a small hanging valley. Surrounded by low lumps of twisted rock, its surface was totally flat, an enclosed meadow of beige and green grasses bright with sunlight and safe from the outside world. At its far end, where a narrow pass formed a natural entrance, two young stags raised their heads from the grazing and, with easy power, turned and were soon gone from sight. Above the opening, a kestrel, momentarily alarmed, wheeled away and took up a new, shivering stance on the air.

Murdo came down off the rocks and walked out into the deep grasses. Below them the ground was wet and gave beneath his weight so that he moved as a man wading through shallows. As he passed out into the meadow he looked up and around and felt himself the centre of a small world.

He paused, held by the feeling of security, of growing confidence. But then he moved on and, as he left the valley, the ground fell steeply before him. It bent downwards in smooth folds of grass before plunging even more steeply into a small gorge where shadows and unlit rock lay beneath an overhang of birch wood. At the top of the wood he passed into a world of dimness and humid air as the hill behind him began to mask off the sunlight.

Across the gorge, the colours were black and olive in the harsh light.

Each tree in the wood was a crippled growth, bent and screwed by the winter winds. The trunks were encased by crumbling white lichen and paddings of moss. And everywhere were fallen trees, half-fallen trees, snapped branches, old stumps, spongy and rotten as they lay in the pools of mud or were slowly submerged by the moss and grasses. Raw wood, bored and pilfered by insect and rot, showed up like old honeycombs in the dank light. The cheeping of finch and tit sounded through the tangled foliage though not a bird could be seen. Further down, still hidden, a sunless burn made its way seawards through the trees.

Murdo lowered himself down the steepening bank, his hands grasping at the pulp and lichen, his boots scarcely finding any hold on the tumble of wet rock, moss and mouldering leaf. Several times he put his weight on the branch of a tree only to lurch forwards as it came away with a dull crack in his hand. It seemed that the whole wood was in a state of final collapse. Even the smells that rose from underfoot were those of death and decay.

He reached the burn, where the water slid sluggishly past barriers of leaves and dead wood; and crossed over, treading his way carefully on the slimy rocks. He felt a sudden revulsion at this unwholesome ditch and started to climb eagerly towards the sunlight above as if he had already forgotten the heat of the open hill.

As he came out of the shadow, his eyes half-closed at the sensation of the sun biting into the nape of his neck. Upwards now he stamped, feet splayed and arms swinging, until he stood well clear of the darkness behind him. Here he stopped, rolling his head from side to side and then sprawled himself out on a bed of rock with his face to the sun. With the warmth rising into him from the rock, he lay for a few minutes, eyes closed, feeling himself suspended in the heat as his ears took in the detailed perspectives of the hill.

Far away, across the gorge, a lamb bleated; nearer, but high in the sky, a hoodie cawed; down below, the burn slid and tumbled; in a tree on the near side of the burn, a chaffinch called. Closer still, a bee buzzed over a cluster of heathers; while just by Murdo's ear, an insect noisily made its way up a crack in the rock. For a while, these simple sounds of the summer hill formed the limits to his consciousness and filled him with a sense of completion and well-being.

Murdo had decided to make for the main road up which he had travelled in the lorry. But though it was only a few hours walk on the road from Drienach, to reach it by crossing the hills was a different matter. He knew this but preferred it for his safety: he was in no hurry, had enough food for several days, and the weather was holding.

Through the early hours of the afternoon he walked steadily inland. He passed up and down across the hills, rough and barren, that lay before him, studded, leather-covered backs. Time and again he was forced downwards by small glens and corries that blocked his path. Undeterred, he made the descent and hauled away up again to tramp on through long stretches of wet ground, to turn and weave his way through the brush-headed towers of peat hags. Birds rose and piped about him, deer broke and fled before his approaching figure, sheep just stared and gaped and returned to their grazing. The sun bowled slowly over towards the shiny, waiting sea, leaving the sky growing heavy and thick with clouds and yellowish haze.

Under this mid-afternoon light, the landscape fell into an almost colourless state. The harling of the hills became banded and spotted with blackness, crags and gullets like smearings of ink; while the shrouding of the sky hung threateningly above, making mere silhouettes of the hoodies and buzzards and smaller birds that passed overhead.

Murdo felt himself being slowly sucked dry by the heat. He was soaked in sweat, his feet were hot and swollen in his boots, his eyes sore with the glare. Crossing burns, he was forever falling to his knees and lapping at the water. And he would take off his boots and bathe his feet till they ached. But the relief lasted no more than a few minutes after which his throat was dry and his flesh burned angrily. There was virtually no escape from the sun for, while it stood high in the sky, its rays struck and lanced down everywhere. Occasionally, there would be an overhanging crag or a steep-sided hollow by a burn where he could lie panting for a while; but otherwise he could only press on relentlessly.

It was around four o'clock, just as he was climbing up a low hill, that he thought he heard a car. He dismissed the idea and walked on. But a moment later the dull groaning buzz came to him again. Puzzled, he hurried to the top and, looking down into a small glen, saw a cart track. He crept down behind a spine of heathers and waited. Gradually the car got nearer and finally, with a roar sounding grotesque after the long hours of silence, a Land Rover nosed into view. It bumped and rolled down the uneven track and disappeared. A while later, its noise suddenly stopped.

Murdo sat on the hillside and looked down at the track and across the glen at the opposite hillside that rose steeply to a ridge. He listened for the car, heard nothing and started to hurry down. When he was three-quarters of the way down to the track, he heard the car coming back. He jerked to a halt, momentarily locked in indecision, and then ran quickly on downwards across the glen.

For all the walking he had done that day, he climbed with remarkable speed. The ground was grassy and firm

110

but it curved steadily steeper as it rose to the ridge. His legs began to ache, his lungs could not get their breath. But already the car was close again. He heard the engine revving, the change of gears, the growling as it rode up a slope, the quicker descent, the increasing closeness. His eyes started from his head, his mouth stretched for breath, his muscles were beginning to fail him. He scrambled and clawed at the grass, beastlike; like a swimmer, his arms reached out before him, pulling and heaving. And as the car started up a short incline just out of sight, Murdo gave one last violent thrust and hauled himself over the top.

It was only a few seconds later that he heard the Land Rover stop below.

Three men stood talking by the car. One of them looked around at the hills and pointed northwards back along the track. Another of them shook his head and gestured towards the west where Murdo lay. The first one shrugged and went round to open the door at the back of the Land Rover while the other two, still talking, turned and faced Murdo.

He waited for no more. Though still panting from the climb, he slid back and fled stumbling over the flattened tussocks and heathers.

If he had not been impelled by fear of pursuit, if he had not thought that the men were already halfway up to the ridge, he would perhaps have paused before the view that was fast opening out in front of him. As it was, he merely glanced at the spreading landscape and came storming downwards, arms flailing, legs pounding, eyes darting hawklike for footholds.

In crossing the ridge he had passed the last of the coastal hills and had broken out into an area of great desolation. Here the hills broke and separated and became closed furrows of rock that rose wavelike, with spurs and arms reaching out to drive obliquely across the lie of the land.

And tucked in the folds of this turbulence, there showed the countless splinterings of water. Small pools lay dotted in the hilltop rocks; lochans, some bare, some fringed with reeds, pushed in close below ragged outcrops; a waterfall, distant, spouted motionlessly, a small stroke of whiteness on grey; and in the foreground, its shores gnawed and torn by numerous bays, the flat sheet of a large loch spread itself dazzlingly in the sunlight.

But all this was overridden by a handful of mountains that, standing quite separately, took on seemingly immense proportions. Their sides pushed upwards in steep rushes and ramps, making cliff and perilous, hanging scree, with castlework of crag and precipice till the dim points of their summits pricked, high and remote, out into the vacant sky.

When Murdo came out on to level ground, he made for the shore of the large loch that lay close by. He splashed through a bed of reeds and went along a sheep track that ran the edge of the loch. From behind a pile of rocks he looked back towards the hill but there was nobody in sight. Feeling himself at a disadvantage in the exposed ground, he went on along the shore, aiming for the confusion of hills that stood beyond the water.

But here the shoreline coiled and sprang about among the hillocks and waterside slopes. He tried cutting away from the loch but found himself blocked by an adjacent lochan. He tried a middle line between the two but, on coming over a neck of rising ground, discovered that the loch here put out a branch some two hundred yards long though less than quarter that distance in breadth.

He stopped and looked down into the water. The stony shore slipped darkly away into deepness. Grudgingly, he walked round this arm of the loch and on into the beginning of the rocky hills but still throwing anxious looks over his shoulder. That he saw nobody gave him little assurance: in the broken contours of the ground it would not be difficult for a man to move unseen.

As Murdo walked this circuitous route, now climbing, now rounding the edge of the hills, the view before him became constantly more dominated by the largest of the mountains. It still stood some two miles away but each time Murdo cleared the top of a hill or edged out along a headland into the loch, a little more of it came into sight.

It rose massively on a double plinth of grassy ground, comparatively free of rock. And it was the gentleness, the smoothness of these two terraces that underlined the ruggedness of the upper mountain. For, rising from the higher terrace, it suddenly reared up a thousand feet sheer in a wall of crag and buttress with the occasional gully hanging ripped and dark. Enormous fan-shaped screes of fallen rock spread out below these gullies, accentuating the towering rise of the great face. Out above the thrust of the wall, the mountain levelled off and climbed more leisurely for another five hundred feet before bursting skywards in a pillar of rock.

At last the loch began to bend perceptibly towards the west. By now the sun was low over the hills from which he had come; and, as in the past few days, the air became thick and humid with the approach of evening.

Ahead of him, he could see the end of the loch. With relief, he started up the spur of a hill which formed a headland jutting out into the water. He came strongly over the top and stopped dead in his tracks. Away to his left, north-westwards, he saw the corner of another loch glinting out from behind a hillside. And the two lochs, a quarter of a mile apart, were joined by a channel of water some fifteen yards wide. He sat down disconsolately and looked at the channel. High out above, the mountain wall stood fierce and ungiving.

He followed the channel back to the loch, peering down

into its dark, still water for any sign of shallows. Then he retraced his steps and passed on towards the other loch. Far down the channel, he came to a place where a spit of gravel, dull orange through the brown water, thrust out towards the opposite bank. Here and there, rocks protruded, giving the impression of a ford. But the water was covered by a skin of brightness making it impossible to see down below the surface.

He walked backwards and forwards, bending down, shading his eyes, trying to get a sighting of the channel's depth. He even waded out along the spit till the water had risen to his thighs; and while the bottom seemed firm before him, the glinting surface still refused to reveal anything. He went back to the bank and stood pondering.

The second loch, though smaller, lay almost parallel to the larger one; so that Murdo found himself wedged far up between the two. To go back was unthinkable. He had not given much thought to the three men for a while but they now presented themselves as an added reason for not going back.

Murdo looked again at the water. It stood dark and still, unknown behind its polished, smiling face. He looked again at the two lochs, knowing in advance that no solution lay in that direction, yet still hoping for some new idea. He bit his lips and rubbed at his sunburnt neck.

Murdo might have remained undecided on the channel bank for quite some time if it had not been for the sudden bark of a dog. Two short barks from behind him and at a distance which was hard to guess in the summer silence. He cocked his ear but heard only the thin call of a meadow pipit. He tried to persuade himself that it was a fox he had heard; yet knew well enough that it was a dog.

Quickly tying his thornproof to his piece-bag, he flung the bundle over the channel where it landed heavily in some heathers. Then with a quick glance behind him, he waded out again along the spit.

The water rose up around his thighs, cold and gripping even after the heat of the day. Higher it rose and higher as he edged his way further out, feeling the bed before him with an exploratory foot. Nearing the middle of the channel, he reached out and touched nothing. Trying again, he reached out and downwards till the water was above his waist. He touched the bottom, firm rock, and remained frozen in this awkward straddling position while he decided what to do next. Gingerly he drew his other leg forwards until both feet were together and the water was lapping at his stomach. He was now in the middle of the channel.

Once again, he reached out tentatively with his right foot but it flapped about without touching anything. He stood with sweat prickling out on his forehead. Again his right foot reached out, but further. And his left foot slipped.

He gave a small, muted cry like a child and went down with a rich plumping sound, one arm just having time to beat at the surface in search of a hold before the cold water closed over his head. He saw a flurried mass of bubble and light undershadowed by the darkness below. His head was filled by a great booming, a hissing and the noise of his own body as his throat opened and closed in useless gulps. His hand struck something but it was already gone and he was being buried alive, blinded, suffocated, bound in the darkness.

He kicked downwards and felt his leg sink into a bed of mud without touching the bottom. With the fury of panic, he kicked again, backwards, and struck hard rock. With both feet he lashed out at this rock and rose like a buoy released, breaking the surface in an eruption of tangled water and limb. He just had time to see the sun, spangled with water, and to draw in a deep breath of warm air before he went down again and the coldness closed resolutely over him.

But this time he came down in shallower water on a bed of muddy rock. Feeling himself on the far side of the trench, Murdo propelled himself forwards and came up to find the surface close above his head. With one or two more kicks and a wild paddling of his arms, he found himself in his depth with the water encircling his chest. He snorted and choked, coughed and spat and rubbed the water from his eyes. Like a great beast of the river, he made his way slowly towards the bank where he hauled himself out, heavy and bedraggled.

He stayed kneeling on the ground, hands on thighs, his breathing slowly calming. He looked back at the water and already it had resumed its innocence, with only the slightest trembling of its surface revealing what had just happened. Murdo sniffed twice, sneezed and looked round in amazement as if only now realizing what had happened.

He got unsteadily to his feet. Putting the bag and coat over his shoulder, he looked back over the channel. Nobody in sight. He turned and started off, keeping the now westerly sun directly behind him. His boots squelched and sucked; his trousers stuck to his legs.

After he had been walking for a while, Murdo realized that he would soon need to find a place to spend the night. With the mountain before him, he decided to make for the lower terrace from where he would be able to keep watch over the surrounding countryside.

It was just as the sun vanished behind the hills to the west that he finally came to the foot of the mountain and began to climb the slope to the terrace. The grass above him was already thick with a mixture of honeyed light and swelling shadow. The great wall of the mountain was hidden by the upper terrace but far above could be seen the summit pillar alight with the setting sun.

He came up on to the terrace and, searching round, chose a shallow, bracken-filled hollow for his bed. Having wrung out his socks, he settled down to his evening meal of cheese, a piece of cold meat and some bread.

Below this small figure, the metals of loch and lochan shone with subdued light while in the hills about them, the shadows were mustering. It was only high in the sky where the tracks and bolsters of cloud caught the glow of the hidden sun that the day still seemed to exist. Flying southwards over the hills, four carrion crows, black shreds against the upper light, passed away from the mountain and were soon lost from sight.

CHAPTER SEVEN

As the first light began to rise into the sky, the great bird launched itself from high on the mountain wall. It flapped clumsily once, twice and then, as the space grew under its wings, its heaviness was transformed. It swept along the face before banking away and upwards in a series of tight spirals that brought it with motionless wings to a level with the summit.

It rode the thin air with an effortless command, its wing-tips ceaselessly shifting, altering, adjusting to the minute changes in current and drift that rose lightly from the cliffs below. It swung in two wide circles, the straight line of its enormous wingspan bent slightly upwards at the tips, and then climbed once more in grace towards the exaltation of the dawn light. Far above the peak, it levelled again and was touched by the paleness of the new sun that was now edging over the horizon and washing away the remnants of the night sky.

The eagle circled slowly eastwards into the light. When it stood a mile or so to the east of the mountain, it started to descend in long looping curves towards the water-filled land below. Already it saw the creep and scurry of small animals in the heathers and grasses and quickly came down to its hunting height. With rigid wings, it passed rapidly in towards the lower slopes of the mountain, a dark stroke disguised in the flarings of the light. Two hundred feet below it, a young vixen bolted and was gone; but already it was looking beyond as it closed with the mountain slopes. Sweeping in across the upper terrace, it glanced down and, drawing its wings, fell out of the sky.

The blue hare, nibbling at some moss, knew nothing of

the bird and only paused with ears erect at the sudden rush of wind behind it. Out of its stoop the eagle came like a stone. As its yellow legs, outstretched below it, came down on the hare, it opened its spread of wings and stood on the air. The front talons of one foot closed over the hare's head and the rear one, a terrible dagger, plunged through the fur and tender flesh. Beneath the dark power of the bird, the hare squealed shrilly, kicked once and fell limp.

As the first rays of the sun threw the mountain summit into a spire of flashing light, the eagle placed a foot over the warm body and, bending low, began to rip its prey apart.

Another summer day was starting.

A while later, further along the upper terrace, a small herd of deer, composed of hinds and calves, raised their heads from the grazing as the eagle lifted heavily from the ground and rose against the light. Most of the deer calves were already two months old and learning to be wary of predators. But as the herd started to move, one of the hinds with a late-born calf looked round nervous-ly. The eagle slid in towards them and the herd scattered; but having fed, the eagle had no interest in the deer and so passed on along the lip of the terrace. It saw the huddled form of the man on the level below and then turned towards the cliffs. Gaining height, it lazily made its way along the front of the mountain and had soon vanished from sight.

The sun rose into a sky printed with heavy patterns of clouds. Over the western horizon they stood stacked as if left over from the day before. Under the diffused light, wisps and featherings of mist lay over the lochs and larger waterways. Hanging just above the still waters, they dissolved and reshaped with the morning's growing warmth. Below the banks of opaqueness, the waters were chill and with little sign of life.

It was some birds calling far overhead that touched Murdo's sleeping mind. He opened his eyes, stared for a moment as he tried to place himself and then sat up. He got to his feet and, looking about, slapped his arms across his chest and stamped his feet to rid himself of the coldness that filled his body.

He had woken once in the night, his eyes springing open in surprise. He wondered what had woken him for the silence that covered the terraces was intense. His clothes were still heavy with water. Though numb with cold, he had lain unmoving as he felt himself encircled by the empty night.

He seized his bag and coat and came up out of the hollow in search of warmth. As he walked up the slope of the terrace, he blew into his cupped hands and looked thoughtfully down at the ground. Up on the steep rise to the higher terrace, he was struck by the direct rays of the sun and, there on a knoll, stopped to eat. He walked around as he chewed, stamping, bouncing up and down, his body still numb. His eyes had an eager glint, a vague shine of satisfaction. The warmth entered him and he stood still. Looking out over the land, he stared in enjoyment of the isolation, the security in which he found himself.

But it was as he turned towards the west that his eye was caught by a sudden spark of light on a hillside beyond the mountain. Chewing slowly, he kept his eyes on the spot. A hillside of bare rock and grass. For five minutes he remained motionless, staring before him and was just about to turn away when another sharp flash spiked out of the dull mottle of the hill. It came from below a small outcrop of rock but though Murdo stared intently for several minutes longer, he saw no sign of movement.

As he hurriedly did up his piece-bag, he asked himself if

it was mere coincidence that there should be another person so close to him, yet so far away from any village in the early hours of this August day?

He looked up at the mountain heights and there came to him the idea that if he were to take refuge above the cliffs, he would be able to resolve his doubts. He would lie in wait and watch: from the cliffs' brink nobody would pass below the mountain unseen.

He scanned the enormous bluff and saw a buttress that pushed forwards from the main bulk of the wall. Slipping along the terrace until he was level with it, he saw that a steep gully ran obliquely up behind the mass of rock, right to the base of the band of crags that formed a final bastion to the cliffs. There the gully narrowed and vanished into a dark cleft that sliced in a single stroke to the upper heights.

He walked casually along the lip of the terrace; and then, coming to a deep burn, he dropped down and made off upstream. Once in the protection of the buttress, he left the burn and began to climb.

The ground, thick with heathers, rose gently before him. He walked quickly now, glad of the exercise to warm himself, and after a few minutes passed from the heathers on to the fan of rock and rubble that spilled out of the gully above. As he stumbled over this flood, he glanced continually up and felt the towering mass suspended over him. On his left, the flank of the buttress rose seven or eight hundred feet in a single leap of ragged sandstone where only occasional ledges held whiskers of grass and fern. Before him, the gully was a ladder of light up to the bites and gouges of rusty earth where sluicings of the winter rains had loosened and torn away the grass.

As the slope began to steepen, the main rockfall ended and Murdo moved more easily on the ground of the narrowing gully. He climbed hunched forward, hauling himself with his hands and giving off small grunts of effort with each step. Halfway up the gully, he paused on a shelf of rock.

As he stood bent forward with his hands on his knees, he saw the slope drop sharply away to the terrace below him. Above, the distance to the gully's head appeared undiminished. As he went on, he wondered at the unthinking ease with which he had decided to climb the cliffs. He climbed and paused, climbed and paused, the bursts of progress becoming increasingly shorter as he began to tire. When he rested, struggling for breath, he stood on the gully's slope like an ant hanging on a stone.

After half an hour, he entered the upper part of the gully. The pure, bright light from the early sun funnelled up the narrow opening and he felt himself held in the wrinkle of the mountain's body. Now and again, a dislodged stone would rattle and bounce away down. Each scrape of his boots, each grunt as he climbed seemed sharp-edged in the high walling of the gully, adding to his awareness of the growing silence of the heights.

And then, drawing level with the top of the buttress, he left the grass and climbed out over the steep rents of earth, loose and treacherous, that hung below the top cliff. At each step the earth broke away in a chute of rock and grit that sent clatterings and echoes downwards behind him. His face was crossed with frowns of effort as he repeatedly slid backwards in his climbing. But he pressed stubbornly on and a short while later, crawling up through the last yards of the gully, he reached the cliff. Here, as he had seen from below, a part of the rock face had split away to form a squat stack behind which a crevice ran sharply up to the open ground of the summit slopes.

Like a thief, he slipped into the darkness of the crevice. A yard or so wide, cold and dank, its bed was a nearly vertical cascade of loose rock, large and small, wedged between the walls. Forty feet higher, at the top of the fall, the sky was a plate of delicate blue fractured by a line of cloud.

But it seemed safe enough and he climbed easily, supporting himself on the walls as he went. About halfway up, he stepped on a rock and felt it give and tip beneath him. He tried to put his weight on his hands but, with a grinding noise, the rock began to go and the rocks immediately above shifted as if they, and all that rested on them, were about to break free. Murdo froze. The movement halted and chill silence poured back into the crevice. Gingerly he moved his weight and leant against the wall. Twenty feet directly below him, the entrance to the crevice framed the long, sunny fall to the terrace. He breathed out in relief as he turned towards the last few yards that separated him from the safety of the cliff top.

A short while later, a handful of snow buntings, fluttering about near the edge of the cliff, were startled into flight by the sight of a small head poking up into the sunlight.

Murdo sprang out of the cliff's hold and felt the sky rising round and about him. He walked up on to the soft, springing turf and small fannings of air breathed at his burning face. He walked westwards towards the far end of the mountain. The ground here was bent in long folds that made easy walking after the roughness of the climb. At the end of the wall, he discovered a small, steep escarpment of smooth grass, edged with a parapet of rock. This escarpment stood like a natural watch-tower and commanded a view of both terraces and the hills over which he had passed the day before. He lay there tracing the route he had taken and could see every detail of the large loch with its twisted shoreline and the deep channel where he had gone down. But though he stared hard and long at the hills, he could see no sign of anybody.

All morning, he kept returning to the parapet to check

on the land below. Sometimes, in the suspicion of his fear, he thought he saw people only to realize that they were odd patches of heather or rock. Once, a sudden movement on the upper terrace, a thousand feet below him, caught his eye: but it proved to be only a scattering of deer passing westwards in search of new grazing.

As the hours wore on, Murdo noticed the changes in the sky. The clear brightness of the early morning sun was long gone. The sun itself was now only a patch of gathered glare behind the clouds. In spite of the height, the air on the cliffs was heavy and stale and as he lay peering out over the rocky parapet, he kept licking his lips and blinking against the sticky heat.

Down below, the features of the land had fallen under a smoky light. Colours dulled, perspectives were flattened, distances became indeterminate. The tracts of water glinted dully among the grey-green pottage of the hillsides. A wooded island far away in the corner of a large loch looked like fretwork in metal. The herd of deer that had grazed the terraces earlier in the day had moved off and the only remaining creatures were the few sheep that lay on the hills like maggots. When one of them cried out, its voice sounded throttled and distant, giving Murdo the feeling that the mountain was being slowly isolated, cut off from the surrounding countryside. Once or twice a hoodie flapped its way silently round the mountain's base: but otherwise everything seemed to have succumbed to the weight of the heat.

Not long after midday, Murdo came down from the parapet. In the hours that he had watched over the countryside, he had seen absolutely nobody. The disappointment of his plan failing, the lack of certainty as to what he should now do and the stifling heat had all accumulated and combined; so that now as he ambled aimlessly about on the slope, he kicked at tussocks and stared moodily down at the ground. What had seemed so obvious and sensible six hours earlier, now seemed both pointless and stupid. What was he doing by himself high on a mountain in the middle of nowhere? Here he was, running like a beast, living on his wits, planning from moment to moment – and all so that he could get away to a life that as yet did not exist . . .

He lay there on the grass thinking with horror of the futility of his existence. He suddenly felt too old to be running, too old to be fighting for survival. He was tired. The only reasonable thing to do was to give himself up and accept the consequences.

As the great layers of cloud and heat piled up over the land, Murdo's thoughts turned to Dougie. It was perhaps the boy's bright-eyed enthusiasm, his innocent optimism that made Murdo think of him with such pleasure, seeing in him all that he himself was now lacking in the wiltings of age. Yet it was not Murdo's body that reminded him of the passing of his middle age, for his job had kept him strong: it was more his mind in which there was the incessant temptation to surrender, to fall passive, dependent on the chance fluctuations of circumstance for everything. Although the long years of his marriage had forced him into a state of resignation, he had never quite lost the urge to fight. Indeed, it had been a violent convulsion of this spirit that had finally caused him to leave. Yet it was as if the very effort needed to effect his escape had drained him of his last strength, so that now, some three weeks later, he was like an old man devoid of interest, even in his own life.

Lying on the grass in the hot silence, Murdo soon fell asleep. His short night's rest, chilled and wet from crossing the channel, followed by the struggle up the mountainside, had left him tired. He felt the stalking approach of sleep but just let himself be taken. There was no hurry now: he had all the time in the world.

All through the dragging hours of that afternoon, the clouds compressed themselves into bank and coiled bank of yellowish tension and power. The light began to fail prematurely, throwing the landscape into an unnatural dimness under which the strakes of water lost their sheen and became slabs and parings of grey. And with this strange light came a silence even deeper than before. The sheep cowered motionlessly; not a bird was to be seen. Crushed by the immense ponderous heat, the earth gave off smells of heather, grass, bog-myrtle, moss and peat with a new pungency that cloyed the air with a heavy richness.

The day hovered in this state for a further hour or so with no return of the light nor any release in the hidden pressure. At one moment, late in the afternoon, the eagle sprang into view, curling up high above the mountain's peak. Once again it looked down on the sleeping man's form and then soared away upwards till it hung, a faded span of darkness, nearer to the clouds than to the mountain's top.

Suddenly it grew darker. The tension that had been gathering in the air over the past week, tightened itself still further and hung poised in instability. From time to time, quiverings of lightning slipped out, uncontrolled, away to the north-west. Around the mountain, the sense of the impending tumult remained undisturbed.

For a while longer the lowering mass of the sky was held in suspension. The undersides of the clouds were lined and pock-marked with blue and brown darkness as if stretched to bursting point. Beneath them, the hills were completely two-dimensional, shapes of blue-grey board slotted about in the land at random. Away in the distance, the flickering continued ceaselessly.

And then, quite suddenly, somewhere out towards the coast, the sky split in the first roll of thunder. It was a startling, vibrant sound after the hours of silence, growing from the lightest fingering of a drum to a moment of cavernous anger before it subsided and petered out. For half a minute, the weight of silence returned almost as if the moment of thunder had been a mistake. But then, after a renewed flurry of lightning, the thunder came again, more boldly, seeming to assert its power. Like a herald of the coming storm, it sounded out in several rolls of rising strength that overlapped and covered the land. Once again, a brief moment of silence followed; but it was a silence filled with expectation beneath the storm sky's strength.

In the last seconds of the quiet, a turbulence passed across the hills. Briefer than a wind, it came and went as if it were a mere displacement of air caused by the thunder that followed. For the sound that severed the silence did not roll forth but burst out of the clouds with an explosive crack, a violence that seemed to tear the sky open. And its bursting grew into barrages of wooden booming so that echoes sprang about in confusion in the surrounding hills.

With this first blow of the storm, the small figure of the man high up above the mountain wall jerked up. Murdo, sleeping long and deep in the clasps of exhaustion, had been unaware of the gathering darkness of the storm. This first thunderclap threw him so sharply from his sleep that he was already sitting bolt upright when he awoke. And in that second of waking he was thrown from a dream of sun and cool wind to find himself hedged in by half-darkness and the low-slung, thundering sky. He looked quickly up and around and saw that it was too late either to make a descent of the cliffs or to try and cross below the summit. Putting on his hat and thornproof, he buttoned himself up to the neck and crouched down beneath the rocks.

Slowly the volleys of thunder drew in over the mountain top. Every few seconds the countryside was soused with light as the lightning broke from the charged banks of cloud. Whole stretches of hill and water brightened under the flat light, the lochs springing forward dead and milky below the hills where the blandness was cut by the dark clefts of burns. And in the ensuing blackness came the snap and resonant bounding of a thunder-burst from just above the mountain. Even before the echoes had finished tumbling about in the hills, the lightning had jagged again; so that with the storm directly overhead, the noise was woven together into an impenetrable blanket of sound.

Murdo sat looking up at the dim shapes of the clouds, feeling foolish at having overslept and so missed his chance of getting off the mountain. High up on the cliff's edge under the storm, he felt himself more remote than ever before. The noise of the thunder was deafening, crackings and explosions sounding as if the mountain itself were coming apart. Lightning flaring across the face threw the crags and crenellations at its edge into silhouette: while the long, grassy slopes and the summit were awash with light.

For half an hour or so the storm racketed overhead with no sign of moving on. Murdo began to have the sensation of being trapped inside it, of being cut off from the outside world. He thought of the morning's silence, the hot stillness in the gully, the long dream of peace he had had . . .

Gradually an anxious impatience began to build up within him. At one moment, as if to calm himself, he shouted something up at the clouds but his voice was smothered by the noise and he slumped in resignation. But only a while later the storm began to drift away towards the south-east. For a long time yet both the lightning and the thunder continued to work angrily over the hills but then it all subsided into soft drum-rolls and guttering lights far off in the distance.

But though the thunder had passed, no light returned for by now the day too was finished. Touched here and there by a flittering wind, the old silence fell back across the land but brought with it a sense of further expectation. And then, as the first drops of rain fell fat and oily, the wind ceased. Out of the still air, the rain began to thicken. It fell heavily, in a vertical mass unswept, unturned by even a breath of wind. It fell with a concentration of power, kicking up the dusty surface of the peat, prickling at the lochs and pools and bouncing off the rock.

Up on the mountain, there was no escape for Murdo. So he just remained sitting by the rock with his head drawn down to his shoulders and his knees pulled up beneath him. The rain drummed on his hat and coat with monotony. Unlike the normal mountain rainstorm where the ascent of wind through the corries and across the ridges sweeps the rain in curtains and spouts, this rain simply dropped out of the sky with such weight that Murdo felt himself assaulted, battered by it. Just as the long-drawn thunderstorm close over his head had brought him the sensation of being trapped, immensely remote, so too this heavy rain, unseen in the darkness of the early night, seemed to blanket out the idea of his other life. It was something that had happened, that he had been part of . . . but so long ago that it no longer had any relevance. Now, the only relevance was the darkness, the rain, the great cliff behind him, the whole night stretching ahead.

His mind was wandering, lulled by the rainfall's changeless beat. By now the water had collected in the folds of his coat and hat so that the slightest shifting of his body sent sluicings of it into his clothing.

The rain continued unabated for more than an hour. Then Murdo raised his head as he felt it slacken slightly. It thinned and lightened and finally stopped; but then after swithering for a while, suddenly began all over again. This second cloudburst at one stage reached such a pitch of ferocity that it struck Murdo with the force of hail. It ended as abruptly as if a shelter had suddenly been placed over his head. One or two more heavy drops bounced off his hat and then, announced by a breath of wind, the passing of the storm was complete.

Murdo got to his feet and stamped about in the darkness. After the afternoon heat, he now felt crippled by cold and exhaustion. He kept moving about for as long as he could and then took a rest by the rock. Finally, out in the small hours, he sat down once more and almost immediately fell into a fitful sleep.

With the first glimmerings of the dawn light, the mountain top withdrew into a huddle of cloud and once the sun rose to the lip of the horizon, this became permeated with brightness. On the slopes below the peak, the ground lay under diffusions of gauzy whiteness. The cloud glowed and everywhere there was sparkling wetness.

Murdo lay half-turned against the rock. He had seen the growing pallor as the sunlight slowly came down on the cloud and had meant to get up and leave. But in his feebleness he let himself be washed back into sleep.

Something warm and wet brushed across his nose. He opened his eyes and found himself face to face with a dog. In amazement he sat up and the dog swung away at the violence of the movement and stood looking at him from a distance. But Murdo knew the dog and swivelled round as he heard the footsteps behind him. Out of the illuminated cloud came the figure of a man.

'So there you are!' The greeting was warm and natural. 'Are you all right? You'll have had a bad time of it in the night.'

Murdo staggered to his feet and stood swaying dumbly, searching for words. He wanted to ask questions, to have the security of answers and sureness but his head was filled with dizziness and humming. His whole body ached and was as tremulous as a floating bog. He opened his mouth but just one word came out.

'Hector!'

The tall man, standing against the ever-brightening cloud, saw Murdo stumble and stepped forward to steady him.

The dizziness passed and Murdo glanced up at the man. Dampness glistened in the wings of Hector's white hair which was filled with light like the cloud. His large eyes looked down on Murdo without either question or hurry. His arm beneath Murdo's elbow felt as firm as the rocks.

'How did you know I was here?'

Murdo's voice was small and creaking. But the larger man just smiled. Murdo hung his head, no longer able to understand.

'Listen now, we'll need to get you down. There's an easier way over on the north side.'

Hector led the way through the cloud which was already beginning to be holed by light and warmth. They traversed the slope and gradually the ground before them began to bend downwards in a long arc of grass. Going slowly with the dog weaving about them, they began to descend.

On the northern side of the mountain, there were high turrets of rock in between which the grassy slopes swept downwards without interruption. Even as they passed this line of rocks, Murdo looked down through the cloud and caught a glimpse of blue water, far below, startlingly coloured among the flattened half-tones on this side of the mountain. A moment later the two men and the dog stepped out of the cloud and found themselves in brilliant sunshine. Away to the north, other mountains held caps of cloud but otherwise the sky was clear, an unblemished band of milky blue. At their feet, the land was scattered with lochs.

'How are you doing?'

Hector had turned to see Murdo staring vacantly out into space.

With the achings of fever and exhaustion gaining over him, Murdo stumbled on unaware of his actions. Later he was to remember little other than odd views, bursts of light and colour, sensations of floating and the repeated resonance of Hector's voice by his side. Eventually they came off the steepness and followed a rough path that led out of the mountain's shadow and down to a loch where several islands, heavy with small birches, rested on their reflections.

As the path rose up over the shoulder of a hill, Murdo stopped dead. Something in the dimness of his sleeping mind told him that he could not manage even this short climb. He heard Hector speak.

'Come on now – you're almost there. Guisachan's just over the hill.'

But Murdo just stood blinking, staring at the path before him. Hector looked at him for a moment and then, taking him firmly under the arm, began to help him up the slope. When he faltered, Hector bent down and slung the smaller man over his shoulder; and stamping on over the top, they passed out of sight.

CHAPTER EIGHT

The loch that lay directly to the north of the mountain was called Loch Airigh na Beinne. It was set in a broad opening where there were several long slopes of good grass and little rock. Running from north-west to south-east, it was roughly oval in shape and while its northern shoreline was cut with bays and creeks, the low ground to the south edged the water in a long, unbroken sweep of grass and brick-coloured sand. It was up towards its western corner that a cluster of wooded islands lay flat and still on the surface like swollen water-lilies.

Guisachan, the building which stood out in the middle of the curving southern shore, had been preceded there by other, humbler, habitations. At the end of the last century, the men down by the coast had been accustomed to send their beasts and women up to the loch for the summer grazing; and so a shieling had been built, a rough construction of rock and turf. Later, when the land had become part of one of the large estates, the shieling had been replaced by a larger and sturdier bothy to be used by the men who came out to the hills for the deer, the grouse and the ptarmigan. But the game declined and when the sportsmen could no longer be bothered with the six-mile tramp up from the big house near the coast, the bothy fell into disuse for a while before being given over to the estate shepherds as a refuge.

Among these shepherds had been Hector's father and, later, Hector himself. And when, as Bessie had related to Murdo, the estate collapsed and the land was split up, nobody had been particularly interested in an old hut that stood far out in the hills, unapproached by either road or track. In fact, in the sale of the estate houses and more valuable coastal land, it had simply been forgotten. So now, some eight years later, it was few people who remembered its existence and even fewer who knew that Hector Ruarach used it as his own when he made his summer excursions to the hills.

The original bothy had been a dry-stone building with a rough roof. But at some stage in its life, the walls had been repaired and mortared while the roof had been felted and tarred. It was a low, single-roomed house with a heavy wooden door and two small windows that looked out over the shore. Standing as it did in the open, it would have seemed bleak if it had not been for a small but dense patch of pine trees that grew round the back of the building. They were old, tough trees and would have reached a good height by now but for the winds that rampaged across the hills. Nevertheless, they grew thickly and so provided good protection from the south-westerlies.

Murdo slept for most of that day once they had come down off the mountain. He lay curled up beneath the blankets on an ancient, wooden-framed bed, his face pallid and lined. Near the middle of the day, he woke and Hector gave him a bowl of soup and some bread. Neither of them spoke much and as soon as he had finished his meal Murdo lay back and once more fell asleep.

Through the afternoon, Murdo came up from his sleep, awake for a moment before falling under again. Some times the room was empty, at others he would see the man standing in the doorway, his figure vast against the light. But it was well into the early evening before he finally awoke and sat up. Sitting on the edge of the bed, pulling on his trousers, Murdo realized just how tired he had been. Clad in his dry, brittle clothes, he walked out of the bothy to find Hector sitting by the water with his dog. Coils of blue-brown pipe smoke hung over his head.

'So you've had a wee sleep then?'

'Aye, that I have,' Murdo laughed.

He sat down on the grass, soft and warm. The sun was well down behind the mountain but enormous spokes of its light thrown up into the clear sky kept the twilight at bay. The water pattered at his feet. A light wind chased itself across the loch and brushed through the pines by the house.

The two men sat there in silence watching the day go down. Murdo felt that there was talking to be done; but such things had their time and could not be hurried. The dog wandered about for a while and then came and sat by Hector with its pink tongue lolling. The soft, regular panting of its breath, the suck and release of the pipe's smoke and the workings of the evening wind were the only sounds. For Murdo, there was the sensation of having passed through the ordeal and arrived in safety. He knew that this was not really true, that Guisachan could only be a stopping place; but after the two nights out, he found comfort in the strength of the house and the man beside him.

Later, when the night was beginning to creep out across the sky, they went indoors and Hector set about lighting the stove while Murdo trimmed a small oil-lamp and hung it from a blackened hook in one of the rafters. Beyond the range of the lamp, the room was gradually filling with darkness and the windows were no more than stamps of paleness. The peats fizzed and smoked behind the panels of the stove door and soon the whole bothy was tinged with their smell. From the supply of tins which he kept in the bothy, Hector heated some food and added some potatoes from the small patch beside the house. When they had finished eating, they sat by the stove under the lamp's wavering light and drank tea from large, enamel mugs.

When ever they had spoken, it had been in undertones, briefly, as if reluctant to break the encircling peace of the night. Now, with the daylight long gone, with his body fed and rested, Murdo glanced over the top of his steaming mug at Hector. The man sat bent forward with his elbows at his knees, staring at the dull glow of the stove. His large hands dwarfed the mug they held. His eyebrows were raised, wrinkling the shine of his forehead and bald head, his upper lip pulled down so that his long moustache seemed to grow just above his chin. It was a look of enquiry and wonder.

Murdo's head was so full of confusion that he did not know how to start. But in the end it was Hector who spoke, turning from the stove with a smile.

'You'll be wondering how I came to be on Sgùrr na Gaoithe this morning . . .'

'Aye, well I suppose I was.'

Hector, smiling to himself, opened his tobacco pouch and began to fill his pipe. It was only when it had been carefully packed and the first thick drifts of smoke had risen around his head and climbed into the upper darkness that he spoke again.

'Well, you see, for a while I'd been thinking of coming out to Guisachan for a day or two. But I didn't like the feel of the weather, it coming up for a storm and all, so I thought I'd wait till it had cleared. But then Bessie came over, all bothered like, saying you'd just gone off without a goodbye or anything. She didn't like to think of you going off like that and was saying that if you'd waited a day or two you could have got a lift south with Jimmy Macleod who was taking one of the lorries down . . . Well, you know how women are.'

Murdo smiled.

'Anyway, I decided I might as well get away to Guisachan, storm or no storm, and that if I came out on the road

136

I might well walk part of the way with you. But when I was past the village, I didn't catch a sight of you for a long while and then you were a good way ahead of me. I had the glass on you and when you left the road and started up the hills, I couldn't think where you were off to, for there's nothing up that way for miles. Anyway, a while later I got a lift with some of the Forestry Commission boys who were going out on the old road to Achnangart to have a look at some land that was to be planted.'

'How many of them were there?'

'What? Oh, just the three of them . . .'

'In a Land Rover?'

'Aye. Why do you ask?'

Murdo shrugged and shook his head.

'Anyway, as I was saying, I came out with them. They put me down about a mile from Achnangart and when I got up on the hill what did I see but you going a hell of a speed along by the loch. You looked as if you were running for your life.'

'I thought I was,' said Murdo with a laugh.

'Well, I couldn't make out what you were up to. It's hard going out there and easy enough to lose your directions. There's nothing out here but the house till you get to the main road about ten mile away so I thought I'd just see what you were after. And the way you were going, it'd not have surprised me if you'd gone and taken a bad fall. And then where'd you have been?'

Murdo, gazing at the stove, was only half-listening.

'So I went away northwards thinking that I'd be bound to come up with you by Loch nan Uidh because I knew you'd have to come back that way when you came to the channel. Well, I waited long enough but I never saw you again till much later when I caught sight of you through the glass under Sgùrr na Gaoithe. How the hell you got there without passing me I really don't know.'

Murdo gave a small snort of amusement.

'I crossed the channel,' he said.

'How did you manage that? Can you swim?'

'No, I just . . . sort of waded across.'

'Away! It's deep enough there.'

'Aye, so I found out.'

'Well, well. . . so you got across, did you? Anyway there was no catching up with you that night so I bedded down in one of the caves above the loch and thought I'd just wait till the morning. Well, the next day I caught a glimpse of you going up into the cliffs. Again I couldn't think what you were up to so I just came round to see if you were going to cross over the top and come away down this side. But you didn't appear and then later I saw you on top of the cliffs. Anyway I'm thinking it was just as well that I did follow you.'

'Aye,' said Murdo. 'Aye, so it was.'

For a while, a silence slipped between them. Murdo hoped that Hector was going to say something about the police coming out to Camascoille. But Hector just sat there puffing at his pipe and absent-mindedly rubbing his knee with the palm of his hand. At one moment a fox barked in the distance and Hector's dog pricked up its ears. It sat there alert for a while and then dropped its head back on its paws and blinked in the warm light of the stove.

'Did you hear how Dougie was doing?' Murdo ventured.

'Och, he'll be fine, don't you worry. I was over early in the morning you left and he seemed much better already.'

'You came over, did you? I didn't see you,' said Murdo innocently.

'Aye, well I'd come across to see Bessie because there'd been some trouble with the police at Drienach.'

'Oh?'

'Ach, I think Alec had taken the accident with Dougie badly . . . Anyway, he'd got a hell of a drunk and there'd been some kind of a fight outside the hotel. I don't know exactly but somebody got hurt and the police were wanting to see him . . . You know how Alec can be when he's taken a drink or two.'

'Aye, or so I hear . . . And that was all they were wanting?'

'Who, the police? Aye, so far as I know.'

And so the conversation came to a close. Not long afterwards, with the stove's heat falling and the beginnings of a night wind running over the ridge of the roof and into the trees, they went to bed. Insisting that Hector should take the bed, Murdo made himself a rough couch of coats and blankets on the wooden floor. A moment later, the lamp was out and the darkness of the hills was complete.

Murdo lay on his back staring up into the roof. What a fool he was! He had imagined everything . . . He lay frowning in the darkness for a while and then fell asleep.

When Hector left, a day or two later, he told Murdo that he could stay at Guisachan as long as he wanted. After their conversation the first evening, there had been no reference to Murdo's flight from Camascoille nor indeed to why he had come to be on Sgùrr na Gaoithe in the storm. But to explain this he would have had to tell him everything and he was reluctant to relate his story of guilt and despair to the man. For Hector seemed to Murdo to live in a kind of innocence and peace where hatred and the shabby perversion of happiness that Murdo's marriage had become, would have appeared ugly and despicable. But on the afternoon before Hector left, while they were out digging potatoes in the vegetable patch, Murdo's whole situation was briefly and strangely touched upon.

The tall man suddenly straightened up from his work and stood looking at a large potato that he was juggling in his hand.

'When I was a boy, I mind hearing my father telling my

139

mother a story about a Drienach man who had got himself married to a girl from the Outer Isles. It happened that the girl was a hell of a one for nagging and getting at her man and he was forever telling his friends that he'd made a bad mistake in marrying her.

'Well, one day he just upped and went. Vanished. And the girl, who'd always been so hard on him, now turned round and was in a terrible state saying that she couldn't live without her man and all that. Well, time went by and there was no news of him and she began to quieten down and mentioned him less and less. After about eighteen months, she went back home to the islands where she started going with one of the local men.

'And then, lo and behold, two years later, her husband comes back to Drienach for her. He'd been away to sea and had taken a bad go of some disease in foreign parts and was so poorly he'd had to leave the job. So there he was back in Drienach asking for his woman after all that time and saying that he'd missed her so. And when he heard she was away back home and was set up with another man, he sort of . . . sort of gave up. Well, eventually he got himself some easy work somewhere in the village and went to live in a caravan out along the road. I mind seeing the man though I was too young to understand why he looked the way he did.

'Anyway, it was about ten months later that he didn't turn up for work one day. It was only in the evening that one of the lorry-drivers found him up in the old quarry. He'd driven up there on his motor bike, tied one end of a piece of string to the brake pedal and the other to the trigger of a rifle, put the end of the barrel in his mouth and pressed the pedal with his foot . . . He who couldn't get away from his woman fast enough!'

'What a terrible business!' Murdo said slowly, looking at Hector.

Hector, still juggling the potato, stared back at Murdo and then smiled.

'I was just thinking that there's never much sense in running . . .' he said.

A silence came down between the two of them. Murdo kicked at the loose earth and picked at a scab on his ear.

'No.' He spoke slowly. 'No, I don't suppose there is.'

The next morning Hector was up early. He showed Murdo where everything was and told him that if he cared to use the old boat, he could be sure of catching some good fish. He said that he would be up again in about a week. Murdo had some money left and held out a few pounds to Hector, asking him to buy some food to replace what would have gone from the supply in the bothy.

'No, no! You don't owe me anything. I won't hear of it.'

'Come on now, Hector, take it . . . Listen then, I'll tell you what. Use a bit of it for some food and buy us a half-bottle with the rest. If I'm away by the time you get back, it can go in the cupboard. It'll always come in useful.'

The two men laughed and Hector, calling his dog, turned and went over the hill.

The following days which Murdo spent alone at Guisachan were full of a remote peace for him. With the storm, the weather had changed. The long stifling days of the previous weeks were now replaced by soft, bewildering weather where light winds and cloud-spotted skies chased in after the bursts and flurries of drizzle and greyness. With the falling of the sun, a wind-blown coolness settled over the land, announcing that the end of summer was now not far away.

Murdo spent much of his time out in the boat fishing. He would row slowly up the loch, pausing now and then to follow the flight of a kestrel or buzzard hunting the hills; or simply to feel the boat drifting before the wind. He would sit there with his elbows across the oars, his eyes wandering around over the land with a look of distance and thought.

Up among the islands, he would sit fishing with Hector's old rod, cruising around hour after hour quite unaware of the passing time. As Hector had said, the trout were plentiful and it was rare that he came back without sufficient for his meals. But it was not the fish that kept him out so long for even when he had caught as many as he needed, he still rowed desultorily about. It was only when the sudden arrival of a shower or the turning of a chill wind tapped him back to reality that he started rowing home again.

One day, Murdo landed on the largest of the islands, leaving the boat tethered to a bush. From the water, the island appeared to be covered with a uniform thatch of dwarf birch and alder. But threading his way through the thick growth, he came upon a clearing where there stood a large slab of rock. The trees surrounded him; there was no sign of the loch.

For a long while, he sat there on the rock with his knees drawn up to his chin while the sun passed in and out of the clouds and covered him with streams of shadow and light.

Murdo no longer trusted his own judgment . . . It had all seemed so simple when he left Acheninver. But now, only three weeks later, he could not even remember the feeling of anger that had caused him to set fire to the house; now it seemed nothing but a foolish and quite pointless thing to have done. Why had he not just gone away without being so dramatic? And again, when he had left Camascoille and run for the hills, it had been the same impulsive decision – a momentary panic over a misunderstood conversation – that had caused him quite unnecessarily to take flight and go into hiding.

No, he was not sure what he felt anymore . . . It was perhaps for this reason that he had taken Hector's oblique warning so much to heart and had brooded on it ever since. As he sat there under the sunlight, he went back again to Hector's remark. Aye, it was true, right enough. Already he was tired of running. Now even the thought of Margaret and the idea of their future together began to be a possibility in his mind. With Flora married, there would be less difficulty and jealousy between him and Margaret. They would never be happy together but at least they could try and live in peace which was as much as most other people did. Somehow they would manage . . .

And so Murdo Munro, unaware of the insidious pressures bearing upon his mind, gradually began to persuade himself that to return to his life in Acheninver was the only solution left to him. In the face of the grim alternatives, the great tangle of fear and hate and anger that constituted his feelings for his woman began subtly to be diluted, dissipated by his logic of despair.

As he sat there with the warmth of this decision in his mind, there suddenly came to him the memory of those minutes out on the headland beyond Camascoille. He frowned. He recalled how he had felt the urge to step forwards and so make a clean end to it all. And then how he had passed beyond that temptation and been filled with sudden feelings of deliverance, of deep comfort at the realization that nothing mattered any longer, had perhaps never mattered in the way he imagined; that he had already reached the end and that the future should be one of acceptance. And there had sprung into his mind the idea that if he were only to stop struggling against his life, he could not fail . . . How was all that? Murdo could not remember how such things had come to him: just the reflections on the water and those few disjointed ideas in his mind. Indeed, he had not given it another thought until now when it all seemed to come back to him with a new and unexpected relevance.

For a moment this burst of clarity made him almost light-headed. He lay back on the rock and looked up at the sky, his hand moving over the lichens in gentle rhythms of detachment. But then he remembered the house. If only he could get some news of it . . .

He got to his feet, walked quickly back to the boat, untied it and put off. He rowed back to Guisachan with a new vigour, almost as if he were in a hurry and could not wait to set off for Acheninver and put his new resolve into practice. But by the time he reached the bothy, it was already mid-afternoon so he decided to wait till the following morning before leaving. He would get to the main road, hitch a lift south and then telephone the minister.

He spent the rest of the day in a buoyant frame of mind, going about things with eagerness and even occasionally humming tunelessly to himself. He sawed up the remains of a pine tree, brought in a new supply of peats from the shed, burnt some rubbish and then, when he had cleaned up the whole place to his satisfaction, he went indoors and cooked himself a meal. After he had eaten, he stood in the doorway drinking his tea and watched the stars come up. He felt a strange elation at the thought of the trial ahead of him.

In the middle of the night, he awoke to hear the thin patter of rain on the roof. He was cold. He pulled the blankets up to his chin and, in doing so, remembered that he was going back to Acheninver. Iciness of fear and horror ran across his consciousness. Lying rigid in the vaultings of the night, he could not imagine how he had come to take such a decision – facing Margaret, the house burnt to the ground, all the village watching him? What had he been thinking of? It was just another of his mad blunders . . .

Murdo closed his eyes tight, and gritted his teeth as an onslaught of panic collapsed all his hopes and resolutions.

In despair, he turned away once again from all thoughts of Acheninver and found himself face to face with his other self – a jobless, homeless, friendless old man.

He tried to think of other things. He wondered what the date was and worked out that it must be August 25th. In two days' time it would be his birthday. Fifty-nine was hardly a good age when you are looking for a job . . . And so once again he returned to the old problem. Twisting and turning in this fashion, he lay awake for a couple of hours, pursued by anxiety, and saw the first lightening of the sky before he finally returned to his sleep.

When he awoke, the first thing he heard was the irregular brushwork of gusted drizzle on the windows and roof. Standing shivering by the window, he looked out on low cloud and mist being driven across the hills from the south-west. Across the loch, the outlines of the hills surged and receded among the clouds. To the west, even the islands were occasionally hidden from sight. By the house, a strand of wire was strung with raindrops.

Murdo realized that all he could do was to wait for the weather to clear. But as he paced up and down inside the bothy, occasionally stopping to peer out of the window, he felt the last semblance of his will-power being gnawed away. At one point the rain stopped and, seizing his coat and bag, Murdo slammed the door behind him and set off eastwards into the hills. But he had only been walking for about five minutes when the clouds closed down over him and curtains of heavy drizzle once more began to cover the hills. He waited for a few minutes to see if it would clear again and then, with a curse, he turned and made his way back. For the rest of the day, the weather remained unchanged. By the time he went to bed, Murdo's temper was rough and raw.

In complete contrast, the next day came up bright and clear, with a cool wind running under the sun and everything bursting with reflected light. Murdo woke late but as soon as he saw the sunlight he was out of bed and preparing to set off. Waiting for the kettle to boil, he walked up and down kneading his hands together thoughtfully. He was just setting the bothy in order when he heard the bark of a dog and, going out, saw Hector striding down the slope.

'Hello there, Murdo. How have you been keeping then?'

'Well enough, thanks. But you're hell of an early.'

'Aye, I was away early enough. I managed to get a lift up to the Achnangart road-end. But I'm not stopping long for I've to be back down at Achnangart as soon as I can. I said I'd help Angus with the sheep.'

'Oh aye . . . Well I was just leaving myself. But I suppose we could take a cup of tea . . . I'm sure you'll be wanting one.'

'Aye, I could do with one, right enough.'

While Murdo raked up the embers in the stove, Hector started unpacking the bag of food he had brought up from the village.

'Here you are then. Here's the half-bottle you were wanting.'

'Oh, so you remembered, did you . . . Will you take a wee one?'

'No, not just now, thanks. Oh, I nearly forgot – I've a letter for you.'

Murdo, puzzled, took the letter but before putting it in his pocket, he glanced at the envelope and immediately recognized the writing.

'How did you get this? Did Bessie give it to you?'

'No,' answered Hector craftily. 'I was just on my way over to Camascoille yesterday when I met the postie. I said I could save him the trouble and then when I saw that the letter was for you, I was thinking that it would be easier on Bessie if she didn't know you were up here.'

'Well, I'm sure you were right. It's better that way.'

When they had drunk their tea and talked about the fishing for a while, Hector got up and said that he must be on his way. As he picked up his bag, he turned to Murdo.

'So you'll be going back then.'

'Aye, well I reckon so.'

'Well, I'm sure it'll be for the best . . . Look, Murdo, there was something I was wanting to tell you . . .' Hector looked down at the ground, overtaken by a sudden lack of words. 'You see, I met Mary Matheson the other day and . . . and she told me what a state Bessie had been in over your leaving. You mind how I told you?'

'Aye,' said Murdo glumly.

'Well, it seems that Bessie had heard from your minister . . . I forget his name now.'

'MacFarlane. Walter MacFarlane.'

'Aye, that was it. Well, when you went, she telephoned him and told him that you were on your way back but that you weren't . . . what shall I say? . . . you weren't so well.'

'Oh.'

'Anyway, she asked him to sort of . . . to have a word with you. Well, she asked the man to help you.'

Murdo looked away over Hector's shoulder and saw the summit of Sgùrr na Gaoithe, vast and strong, against the wash of the sky. In the moment's pause, a breath of wind carried the far-off mewing of a buzzard across the air.

'The minister said that it was all a bit complicated. It appears the police are on the look-out for you. He didn't say why. But he said that he'd been hoping you'd try to get to see him as he had an idea that he might be able to help you explain things to them. Well, as Mary said, it was all a bit late, seeing as you were already away. But I thought I might as well let you know.'

'Aye. Thanks.' They stood in silence, avoiding each other's eyes.

147

'Anyway, if you're wanting away, you'll need to make for the bealach between Sgùrr na Gaoithe and the hill on the left. Do you see where I mean? Aye, well once you're over the bealach, keep on east for about two hours and you'll come up with the road. Will you leave the key to the bothy under the stone by the door. I'll be through at Achnangart by tea-time tomorrow so I'll be up here afterwards.'

'Right, I'll do that.'

A short while later, Hector set off. At the top of the hill, he half-turned in his stride and was about to wave but Murdo was no longer to be seen. So he called sharply to his dog and as the animal came bounding back to his side, the two of them passed over the rise and out of sight.

CHAPTER NINE

The hours wore on. Beneath the high, unblinking sun, the morning pulled slowly forwards, still and warm. Insects moved crazily about through the heat-pressed smells that were carried here and there over the upland hills on the eddies of air. Stonechats and whinchats, wheatears and pipits chased backwards and forwards over the heathers and rocks. Some way to the south, an old dog fox trotted leisurely along the bank of a burn; while in the hills beyond the loch, a heavily built wildcat settled itself down to wait in the brackens near a rabbit burrow. Just before midday, a pair of teal flew fast across the face of the sun and were soon engulfed in the sky.

Once the sun had reached its peak and started to descend, the sky began to fill with cloud until the whole landscape was marbled and restless beneath the shifting pattern.

Even from just across the water, the man who sat on the grass was nothing, a scarcely discernible point among the vastness of the land. For a long while, he sat there as if taking the sun, motionless, uninterested by everything outside his own consciousness. From time to time his blue, watery eyes quavered and moved over the surface of the loch. Otherwise he remained quite rigid as the sunlight poured down on him and reflected off the gloss of his head.

When the clouds began to mask the sun, he glanced up for a moment and then, getting slowly to his feet, he started off along the shore. His head seemed sunk into his neck, his shoulders drawn forwards, his movements sluggish as if he were staggering beneath a sack of oats. After going some way up the loch, he sat down again and began to trace shapes in the coarse, reddish sand with his foot. Later, he walked on again with his hands in his pockets. When he drew level with the islands, he looked across at them and thought of his moment of strength and decision only forty-eight hours before. He gave a quiet snort of derision and looked away.

As soon as Hector had left Guisachan, Murdo had impatiently ripped open the letter. Margaret's writing coiled cold and blue across the page.

It was a brief, factual letter. She told him that the house had been gutted by fire, that the police and council authorities had started making investigations and that as they were not satisfied that the fire had started by accident, they had asked to see Murdo. At this point, the minister had intervened, saying that Murdo was away and that he himself was trying to contact him. She had hoped that Murdo would have taken advantage of the minister's kind help as it would have saved her a lot of shame and embarrassment. But, four days ago, as the minister had still heard nothing, the police had formally started an enquiry. She said that Murdo must be sick in his head to have done such a terrible, sinful thing – and on his own daughter's wedding day. She ended by saying that she hoped the Lord would punish him for what he had done to her and Flora. A footnote explained that she had gone to stay with her sister in Selkirk.

Murdo had looked up from the letter, his face tense and dark. He worked out that the police must have started their enquiry a week ago. He read the letter again and then, letting it fall to his knee, he stared out over the brightness of the loch and wished once again that he were dead. And as he sat there, open-mouthed, gazing sightlessly before him, there had started to take hold of him a fear, the basic animal fear of the hunted. For a moment, he had thought of going after Hector; but the shame of his fear, of his disgrace, stopped him and he just continued to sit there with a stony face and a leadened heart. In speeding circles, the thoughts turned and ricocheted in his mind, endlessly growing in scale and complexity. He longed to stop thinking. He wanted to be left alone. But the words of the letter stood resolutely before him and constructed a neatly detailed picture of his predicament.

But by the time he finally got up and started to walk round the loch, the initial panic was beginning to recede, leaving him with a clearer vision of his dilemma. He knew as before that to continue running would only be to postpone his decision. He could either return to Acheninver or . . . or he could take the whole matter into his own hands and put an end to things.

The possibility of killing himself had been running silently through his mind ever since he had left the island. For most of this time it had remained unadmitted and it had only been in the blackest of moments that it had risen to the surface and offered itself. But now it came forward again, darkly and enticingly, speaking to him of all the humiliation and suffering that was otherwise to come. It flaunted itself before him, promising him a complete end to all trouble; and in the chaos of his mind, Murdo felt himself being drawn. On and on he wandered in a trance of horrified fascination, occasionally casting glances at the shore's shelving and the hinted depths of the water beyond.

Then, suddenly the sun broke free of the clouds and, impelled by its touch, he turned to face it. He threw back his head and closed his eyes and for a few seconds managed to think of nothing but the heat blossoming on his face. When, at last, it faded away behind another cloud, he once more looked out on the world and knew for sure that he must go back to Acheninver.

With that last burst of brightness, the day's bloom was over. For now the sun was screened by furrowed fields of cloud that stretched away to the horizon so that everything lay flattened and dull in a monotony of overcast light. Not long afterwards, it began to rain.

The weightless falling of the rain settled on Murdo tenaciously so that dribblings and seepings of wetness soon made their way through his clothes. But he walked on unnoticing, his hands thrust deep in his pockets, his whole body moving like a machine as he gazed wretchedly in on himself and continued to allow his imagination to conjure up all the consequences of returning home. It was as if he were trapped, held in the vice-like grip of a melancholy which forced him to contemplate without respite the very things that were the cause of his dejection. Murdo Munro's nature provided him with a great capacity for tormenting himself.

He passed round the end of the loch and began to make his way back over the rougher ground of the northern shore. From there it took him near on an hour to return to Guisachan. His small figure came creeping across the dull, muddy contours of the lochside hills that were now beginning to vanish from sight as the rain grew steadily heavier. By the time he reached the bothy, he was drenched.

He closed the door behind him and set about lighting the stove. In the murk of the unlit room, he was a half-seen figure as he crouched hunched over smoke and tenuous flame. The only sounds were those of the rain's unvarying beat on the roof and the faint hiss as the peats began to light. The stone walls of the bothy exuded a chill dampness and even when the fire was burning strongly, Murdo felt little warmth in the cheerless room.

He peeled off his sweater and shirt and draped them over the back of the chair to dry. It was as he was wrapping a blanket round his shoulders that he suddenly remembered the whisky. He opened the cupboard and took out the bottle, holding it up against the firelight to see its glow of promise. Then, unscrewing the top, he placed the bottle to his lips and cast his head back. This first draught was long and greedy and he gasped and grimaced as the alcohol bit him in the throat. He drew up another chair to the stove, squeezed a couple more peats into the fire and settled down to make the drink do its work.

Gradually the whisky started to take hold of him. Lying warmly in his belly, it sent out its suffusions of welling oblivion. He was aware of this, aware of the smiling confusion of his mind, aware even that behind it the truth remained the same; yet he felt a strange surge of power in that he could no longer really be touched. Somewhere deep inside him there was laughter though he could not quite manage to break the sullen stupor of his face.

He drew the blankets closer round his shoulders. The rain still drummed on the roof. Glancing sideways, he saw the bland greyness of the sky palpitate. He got up and peered out of the window.

The hills beyond the loch were now only humped shapes. It seemed such a long time since he had walked across them. Then with a surge of displaced memory, he thought of the cold, deep waters and quickly turned away for the bottle.

By now, it was almost completely dark in the bothy. When he took the lamp down from its hook to light it, he discovered that it was nearly empty and so wandered off into the shadows for the can of paraffin. The top of it was stiff and in his exertions to undo it, he spilt some of the paraffin. He swore softly and tilted the heavy container, the drink persuading him that he could manage without

153

the funnel. But more paraffin went on the floor, making a puddle which he left as he lit the lamp and hung it from the hook in the rafter.

In a burst of anger, he seized the half-empty bottle and drank it almost to the bottom. He stood there beneath the little lamp, his eyes bulging and his lips pursed. He swayed unsteadily and with the swinging of the lamp created wild fluctuating shadows that made the whole bothy seem to move. He blinked and rolled his head and grasped the back of the chair for support. He sat down and held up the bottle. Only a finger of whisky left. A feeling of resentfulness turned over in his stomach . . .

Oh, but he was cold! He pulled the blanket tighter round his bony shoulders but there was still a terrible numbness in his flesh. Opening the doors of the stove, he crammed in some peats. With the doors open, the heat released was savage and struck out at his body; and he sat there, rocking backwards and forwards on the chair, his eyes closed, and let the light and warmth pass into him. For a while he remained like this, moving to and fro; and then suddenly, as he lost his balance, the chair slipped and he fell forwards. Instinctively, he thrust out a hand to save himself but in his drunken state he misjudged the distance and his hand glanced off the top of the stove and came down on the actual bars of the fire. With a roar of pain, he twisted himself away and fell into the shadow beside the stove. Only his legs and the white fingers grasping the wrist of the injured hand could be seen by the dim lamplight. Above him, the sound of the rain never paused. The last of the daylight was passing away.

Still fighting the pain, he got up and looked at his hand. Already the flesh was puffing up where a thick weal ran across his palm. His face was twitching and jerking as he tried to settle the blanket back on his shoulders. He paced around and then, draining the bottle, he stumbled over to the bed.

He pulled the extra blankets on top of him and closed his eyes. It felt as if his head were falling through the pillow, as if there were a great weight in the top of his skull while the rest of his body was floating and insensible. Jumbled thoughts of horror moved about in his mind. His hand felt vast and burning. A nausea bunched in his stomach and began to rise upwards towards his throat. For what seemed like several hours, he remained absolutely motionless, only half-conscious yet far from sleep, waiting for the sickness to pass. At last, with the sudden and uncontrollable swelling rushing up in to his mouth, he rolled over and vomited on to the floor.

He fell back, free of the nausea, and gradually the lightness and weakness cradled his body into sleep. His last thought was a vague wish that he would never wake again.

And so it was, far out in the northern highlands, that Murdo Munro celebrated his fifty-ninth birthday.

Not long after, the rain lessened and finally stopped. Seen from across the loch, the glow of the lamp and the fire remained a pale, still mark on the darkness. Not a shimmer nor frozen flash of light came off the water for the sky remained thick with the passing of clouds.

But later the patch of light framed by the bothy's window expanded, wavered fitfully and expanded again.

Murdo moved restlessly in his sleep and cleared his throat. Several times he grunted and coughed and then, with a loud choking sound, he was awake and sitting up. For a moment, he could make no sense of what was going on around him. Then, as he breathed in, the thickness of the air explained itself and at the same moment he saw the scurrying of flames on the floor by the stove.

He sprang from the bed and stumbled through the

smoke towards the door. Even as he flung it open, light
flared behind him as the paraffin caught fire. Drawing in a
deep breath of the cool, still air, he turned and plunged
back in for the water pail. But by now the smoke was
thickening and before he could get to it, he was driven out
again.

He started to make his way round the outside of the
building for the other bucket; but once beyond the light of
the fire, the darkness sent him staggering blindly in the
rough ground. Yet somehow he managed to find the
bucket and was soon hurrying back to where the smoke
was now billowing through the doorway.

The old bucket was so rusted that the water spouted
from both sides as he went backwards and forwards
between the loch and the bothy. But soon hissing steam
was mingling with smoke and finally the last of the flames
guttered and died. For a while yet the smoke kept him out
but as soon as he could, he went back in and threw open
the windows.

He sat perched on a rock weighed down with utter
misery at this new disaster. He imagined Hector arriving
the next afternoon to find the damage and began to think
over just what sort of thanks this would appear to be.

What strange force was it that was hounding him
onwards ever deeper into this despair? By Christ, what
was wanted of him?

Murdo opened his burnt hand. In the panic to douse the
flames, he had used it without concern and it was only
now that he felt the pain. His head reeled from the smoke
and the whisky. And he was cold.

Back in the bothy, wisps of smoke still hung in the air
and by candlelight the atmosphere was ghostly and
unreal. Finding the lamp still intact, he re-lit it and started
to examine the extent of the damage. Holding it high above
his head, he moved about the room, coughing and

croaking. All around the stove, the stone walls were calcined and white. Higher up, tongues and streaks of sooty blackness reached almost to the roof and as he fingered the walls, the mortar crumbled and fell away. Where the paraffin had burnt, the wooden floor was a mess of sodden charcoal and of the two chairs, there was little left other than skeletons of charred strut and rung. The stove doors gaped coldly, revealing a black, spongy mush. Clouded and coaly-skinned, the empty whisky bottle lay accusingly on the floor.

Murdo hung up the lamp and sat down on the bed. He felt crushed by his powerlessness. There was nothing he could do: the bothy was badly damaged and neither explanation nor apology could put that right. He tried not to think of Hector and all his kindness. Now Murdo's sole desire was to get away from Guisachan as soon as possible. He settled himself down to wait for the dawn.

It was a long night. And the very stillness outside added to this vigil which he kept in preparation for the trial of the journey home.

As soon as the sky began to pale, he slipped off the bed. Standing in his trousers, he looked round for his shirt and sweater and then, realizing that they must have gone up in the flames, he simply buttoned up his thornproof to the neck, picked up his bag and hat and left.

Outside, the ashen light revealed the last moments of the sleeping world. The loch, lifeless, was only a block of matt greyness while the dark hills beyond were still confused with the thickness of night.

Murdo walked slowly away from the bothy, gingerly feeling out the ground before him. After the hours of waiting, it was good to be on the move and to hear the sounds of life about him as the burns carried the night's rains down off the hills. Since the accident with Dougie, horror and uncertainty had been accumulating about him.

Although he now trembled at the thought of returning to Acheninver, he was aware of the elation of relief as he set out towards a resolution of all that beleaguered him.

Each moment, the light was rippling out further from the horizon. It rose like a flood-tide in an estuary, relentlessly sweeping in over the flats of the night sky. Occasionally, it came up against dunes of cloud; but soon it had seeped in and around them, penetrated them with its thin warmth so that at last they too were swamped away.

With the daylight spreading, Murdo walked up over the hills towards the pass that Hector had pointed out. But soon the wash of light gathered itself in and its core of power pushed up over the earth's rim with such brilliant radiance that Murdo had to shield his eyes and tack about in his efforts to see where he was going. When he paused to rest and turned his back to the sun, Loch Airigh na Beinne and the pines of Guisachan were already out of sight.

An hour and a half later, having followed Hector's directions, he found himself down by the roadside. The walk down from the pass had taken him by long slopes and open glens where trees grew in thick bunches. Large numbers of deer were still low on the hills at this early hour, and once or twice black grouse had risen noisely from beneath his feet.

In the last half-mile he had heard the sounds of cars and had prepared himself for the journey. Somehow he must get to the minister. It seemed to Murdo that the man of the kirk was his only source of hope. To get to him, Murdo knew that the only difficulty lay in the crossing to the island for it would be on the ferries that the police would be watching for him. He also realized that his appearance would do nothing to help. It was ten days since he had last shaved. In addition, he had a badly swollen hand and was strangely dressed for the sunny weather with his buttoned-up thornproof. He looked much like a tramp.

He ambled off along the road, dropping his eyes whenever a car came towards him. He let a couple of cars pass for he was waiting for the anonymity of a lorry. He tried one truck without success but a while later, a five-ton lorry with a building contractor's name on the cab door stopped and one of the men asked him where he was heading for. When Murdo told him, they said that that was fine as, by chance, they had to pick up some materials at the ferry terminal. With no room in the cab, Murdo clambered up over the side of the lorry and tumbled into the back. With a harsh clank of the gears, the lorry pulled away and the cloud-scattered sky started to move past over his head.

All through that day, Murdo lay in the deep metal pit of the lorry as they sped away from the north. For much of the time Murdo dozed, waking to see the clouds and taut veil of the sky slipping past high above him. In the afternoon, when they were halted once or twice by the mass of summer traffic in the villages, Murdo lay crouched and hidden till they once more got under way.

It was well into the latter part of the afternoon that, peering cautiously over the lorry's side, he began to recognize the land that lay behind the coast from where the ferry sailed. As they came out at the top of a hill and the small complex of the terminal appeared down below them, Murdo rapped on the roof of the cab.

'Could you put me down here? I've to go and see some folk across there,' said Murdo, gesturing vaguely towards a group of houses that stood up above the sea.

'Aye, surely. Just as you like.'

Murdo jumped down and, with a friendly nod from the driver, the lorry went off down the hill.

Out of the glistening waters, the spreading mass of the island lay languidly in the afternoon haze. From the centre of the island, the dim but shining point of A' Mhaighdean thrust upwards into the light.

The end of the road was near.

CHAPTER TEN

The skipper of the small ferry-boat, a large red-faced man whose enormous girth had earned him the cruel nickname of Ploc – meaning a lumpish promontory – looked across the waters of the sound and checked his watch. The sun was far down behind the island peaks leaving the mass of land dense and purpling inside its crown of fire. It was already past the scheduled time for the day's last crossing and partly because of this and partly because he was suddenly prompted by the thought of his tea, he tilted his great weight forwards and spoke a word or two down through the bridge-house doorway. A moment later, with a muffled explosion and a cough of smoke from its exhaust, the deep chortling of the diesel engine announced that the boat was about to sail.

The handful of cars making the crossing were already aboard but on the quayside there was still a sizeable gathering of people, most of whom were planning to join the boat at the last moment. They stood about in loose groups, chattering and laughing, enjoying the last minutes of warmth and light.

The two policemen, leaning against their car on the corner of the quay, were bored. They had hung around the terminal all day watching the passengers on the ferry and now, with the boat's last sailing imminent, they had checked the people present to their satisfaction and were impatient to be off. They turned away to get into the car and as they did so, a rough-looking figure stepped hastily out from behind the shipping company's storehouse and fell in with the people jostling their way to the boat. He manoeuvred about in the small crowd so that when he came to go up the gangway he found himself next to a tall man whose figure effectively shielded him from the policemen.

Murdo had skulked around on the hillside above the shore for hours, watching the ferry pass backwards and forwards across the sound. He had noticed that the policemen were on the alert and so it was only when he realized that the boat was about to sail for the last time that he came furtively down the hill to try his luck. Passing through the small cross-plan of houses which lay behind the quay, he had moved into the cover of the storehouse and waited for his chance.

It was with relief that he at last saw the ropes cast off and felt the boat draw away from the quay. With a light wind shimmering in over the cooling sea, most of the passengers retired to the cabin, leaving only a few people on deck. Using his last money, Murdo bought a ticket from the young man who was going round the passengers and then pulled down his hat and hung over the rail.

About forty minutes later, as the boat passed into the lee of the island, the wind dropped and the water took on a slickness that seemed sinister in the failing light. Here and there, just below the surface, long-armed jellyfish palpitated with the swaying of the tide. With its engine idling, the boat slithered quietly through the water and pulled in towards the pier.

The first thing that Murdo saw was the police car. He looked quickly round at the passengers who were now milling at the entrance to the gangway and prepared to slip off in the same way as he had come aboard. Keeping his head down, he thrust into the crowd and was gradually sucked towards the gangway. As he set foot on the pier and turned sharply away towards the land, he caught a glimpse of the figure and the chequered capband. Walking quickly away, he had almost reached the road when he heard the shout.

'Hey, you there!'

With the instinct of guilt, Murdo turned and saw the policeman coming down the pier and pointing at him. He turned away again and began to run. There was no sound of pursuit and he just had time to wonder if he had made a mistake when he heard the roar of a car's engine.

Reaching the road, he glanced over his shoulder and saw the car coming swiftly down the pier with its headlights on. He sprinted past the row of houses that edged the road and jumped across a ditch and into the brackens at the foot of the hill. The sky was a high, distant paleness. The slopes above him were dark and safe. He began to scramble upwards.

He heard the car come to a halt and a second later the beam of a powerful torch fell on him throwing the brackens ahead into a weird tangle of shadows.

'Munro!'

But without looking back, Murdo stumbled on, climbing away from the light. Fifty feet above the road, he crossed over into the shelter of a small dip and the glitterings of the pier lights were gone. He moved on without pausing, bending right and starting to traverse the slope in a northerly direction. After a while he stopped and listened; but there was nothing to be heard but the clanking and whirring of winches back on the pier. He breathed deeply and set off across the slope.

The night was now quickly filling up every fold of the hill and behind him the sea was drifting off into a gleaming obscurity. But in spite of the darkness, Murdo climbed with a confidence that came from his knowledge of the land he was on. Though he trod carefully enough, searching for each step through the undulations and fields of brackens that lay across the slope, he trekked onwards with an air of purpose. He was not bothered that he had been spotted: he was free on his home ground and he knew that if he cut diagonally inland, he could reach Acheninver without crossing another road. While he remained out on the hills he was safe. He smiled and sniffed and was pleased. It was as if he had completely forgotten the whole purpose of his return.

But in spite of this little satisfaction, he was tired and hungry. As a forester, he had long been accustomed to pushing himself hard, always vying with the younger men in his ability to sustain heavy work with little rest through the hours of the day; and the thought that he would soon be old had never crossed his mind. But the pressure put on him by the rigours of the past weeks had altered all this. The flight from Acheninver had also turned out to be an unwitting flight from middle into old age. The earlier competitive pride of the man had gone: and with its departure, he was without the urge to continue living the way he had been for so many years. Since the evening on the headland beyond Camascoille, he had sensed, if not fully understood, that he had changed. For in those brief moments, high above the sea, far from the rest of the world, the idea of acceptance, of patient understanding had appeared to him as the answer to his soured, angry way of living.

He paused for a while, watching the stars prickling in the sky like soot in a fireplace. He touched at his hand with his forefinger. When he had last looked at it, he had noticed that the puffiness around the wound had increased and that it was beginning to ooze pus. Now it throbbed and ached so much that it felt as if his whole hand and forearm were on fire.

He stood there thinking of the various houses in the neighbourhood. Then, treading carefully, he started off again by the light of the stars. About half a mile further on, he came down the hill and stopped behind a vast thicket of bramble-bushes. Below him, a large straggling house stood set back from the road.

He hung about by the bush, whiling away the time by searching for ripe brambles. He found a few fruit but they were hard and sour and griped his stomach. Meanwhile, he watched the house and could make out the back of a man sitting at a table in the kitchen. At last, the man got up from the table and a few minutes later the light went off and another came on at the far corner of the building. A low, corridor light glowed dully through the glass top of the back door.

Murdo waited a while longer and then, slipping round the bush, crept cautiously down towards the house, hoping that the couple did not keep a dog.

He paused on the lawn at the back of the house. Minutes passed with the stars and the house lights the only signs of life in the night. He edged forwards again and came up to the back door. He tried the handle and the door opened. With the deed begun, he no longer hesitated but walked silently in.

He was in a small porch, crammed with coats and walking sticks and wellington boots. There was a smell of comfortable oldness, of used but expensive things. He passed through and came to the corridor. The bulb threw an aged, yellowish light and as he stood there he could hear the low drone of voices away to his right. He turned to his left and was immediately in the kitchen where the corridor light shone down on a large pinewood table. The table itself was bare but beyond it showed the tall white shape of a refrigerator. Inside the refrigerator, the bright light revealed four deep shelves laden with food. Swallowing hard, Murdo extricated half a cold chicken and thrust it into his piece-bag. He was just casting his eyes over the rest of the food when he heard a door open somewhere in the house and the sound of a voice.

He closed the door quietly, seized the remains of a loaf from the sideboard and hurried back into the corridor. As he turned into the porch, footsteps were coming towards him. He bolted out of the door and vanished into the night.

Up on the hill again, he walked northwards till he came to the edge of a plantation. Against the glimmering star-light, the spires of conifers stood solemnly up into the sky. He sat down on his haunches and began to eat, tearing the chicken apart and thrusting the flesh into his mouth with crumbling pieces of bread. When he had finished, he sighed deeply and, wrinkling up his nose, looked out over the sound. Between him and the scatterings of lights that marked the mainland coast, a fishing boat chugged resol-utely northwards. A car passed by on the road below, the beam of its headlights swinging backwards and forwards across the night as it followed the curves of the land.

A shiver ran down his back. He stood up, stretched and began to feel his way towards the trees. He climbed through the fence and pushed forward into the wood. The trees grew tightly packed and with their branches reaching low down to the ground, it was hard work to move. When he had gone a dozen yards or so in from the fence, he simply sank down and laid himself out on the bed of pine needles.

He lay there thinking over the day. Deeper in the wood, an owl hooted. Vague rustlings and flappings were inter-spersed with sudden movements of wind in the tree tops. Once, the wire of the fence jangled and he stiffened. It jangled again and then was silent. Murdo wished that he had not lost his sweater. But beneath him, the bed of needles was soft and firm and slowly he dozed off. Just beside the plantation, a small herd of deer settled down for the night.

The wind which had started to rise vanished and for the rest of the night hours the air remained still. Cold and uncomfortable, Murdo slept fitfully. He hugged himself and tried to settle lower into the pine needles like a nesting bird: but it was to no avail, for the night wore on and the chill of the small hours came seeping in through the trees. He turned about constantly in an attempt to drive away the numbness but just as the first light was beginning to appear, he dropped off into a brief sleep. He dreamed of Dougie and sunlight; and then, with the effortlessness of dreams, Dougie became his daughter, Flora. He was in the Acheninver shop where Flora worked and though he seemed to queue for hours she would never speak to him. People came and went continuously while he stood silently at the corner of the counter. It was just as she finally turned to him with a cold stare that he awoke with a start.

He rolled over on to his back and blinked. The thin under-branches of the trees formed a ceiling just above his face. Twenty feet higher, some wood pigeons cooed and fluttered in the tree tops and then took to the air with a mad clattering of wings. Peering sideways beneath the branches, Murdo could see the smoky colour of a cloud-covered sky.

Outside the wood, he stood rubbing at the stubble on his face. The clouds, hanging low over the sound and covering the tops of the hills behind him, gave the morning scene a bleakness. A lone gull flew listlessly along the coast.

Murdo pressed his hand and winced as a gush of pus broke out from the edge of the wound. He turned away from the sea and following the fence up the hill, made for the clouds. At the corner of the plantation he went away north-westwards into a large corrie that hung bowl-like from the covered sky. He walked hard and half an hour later his gangly form disappeared into the cloud.

Murdo was intending to cross the great bulk of hills that

stood between the coast and a long, desolate glen which ran up from the south through the centre of the island. Climbing up the glen, a single-track road passed the last of the farms, and, crossing the watershed in a piece of flat, lonely moorland, started down and into the glen beyond. As this glen to the north gradually opened out, the burns of the hills joined together and formed the river which, seven miles later, flooded through the reeds into the sea-loch at Acheninver.

The clouds coiled and wreathed about the ground, distorting distance and direction, making shallow hillsides seem to fall away precipitously, giving a lone yowe monstrous proportions as she cropped the grasses by a burn. Rocks loomed vast out of the mist and then were gone again. A half-seen wall, only yards away, was sucked back into the cloud and later turned out to be no more than a row of stones. Everywhere there was deception and deathly silence, broken only by the stifled churning of burns or the unowned cries of sheep. Every stem and stone dripped with wetness.

He walked at a measured pace, moving along under walls of dripping, moss-bound rock, following sheep tracks beside the waters of sullen lochans, endlessly casting about for landmarks as he climbed steadily higher. Only once did he seem mistaken and, doubling back on his tracks to a burn he had just passed, he set off again further to the north.

Then, at last, he felt the touch of a light wind from the west and knew that he was near the top. He came out on to a bleak stretch of ground where slabs of rock lay loose on earth and grit. Here the wind pushed the clouds across the rocks towards him in a slow procession so that the small plateau seemed to be sliding forward beneath his feet. He wiped the dampness off his beard and hurried on, now suddenly impatient to be out of the clouds.

As Murdo came down and saw the hills running on into the glen, the feeling of detachment from his journey's purpose fled from him like a bird peeling away before the wind. Passing over the ridges in the cover of the mist, the transition from the outer world to that of his home ground had been made in a state of numbed disbelief. But now, as he looked down on the inland glens of the island where he had spent all his life, he realized that his journey was drawing to a close, that ahead of him lay only reality. As so often before, his strength and hard-won resolution suddenly fell limp and useless at the prospect. In the end, it was sheer exhaustion that drove him on, the weakness of his body dulling the fears of what he would have to undergo.

It was well after midday when he found himself in the glen. The small white farmhouse lay half a mile away, over by the road. A dog began to bark as he approached but since there seemed to be nobody about, he climbed into a field and scraped up some potatoes and a neep.

At the farm's refuse tip, he found an old biscuit tin to serve as a makeshift saucepan. It was at the same time that he happened to turn up a piece of mirror and saw his face, as prickly as an old gooseberry with bloodshot eyes and grey, sagging skin. He tossed the glass away in disgust and made off with the tin towards a small birch wood that grew on the moor at the head of the glen.

Up there he made himself a fire and cooked the vegetables; and when he had eaten, he lay back by the fire and watched the sweet, bluish smoke rise and dissipate among the trees. Nearby in the wood, a bird trilled softly.

He lay there for a long time, enjoying the sensations of the food and fire and dreaming back over things just as if he had come to the end of his life. He wondered vaguely when he would next be able to lie back and listen to the world going by. Then he got to his feet and, kicking out the fire, walked out of the wood and across the moor.

With the summer days beginning to shorten, it was nearly dark when he reached the slope above Acheninver. The worst of the waiting was over. He was back. Had he really ever left . . .?

But now his mind was taken up with the problems of getting to the minister without being seen. All he wanted was the sanctuary of the minister's house where he was sure that he could find both understanding and advice. Had the minister himself not written so to Bessie? He would wait for nightfall and then get down to the back door of the manse.

He laid up in a thicket of gorse and watched the village sink under the incoming night and the first lights going on in the houses below. Margaret would still be in Selkirk, of that he was sure. But he feared to see his daughter: he wanted her to have no part in his disgrace. And he felt his mouth tremble at the sudden thought of her.

He saw some of the other people out in the street and watched them with hard, angry eyes. It was a strange feeling, lying hidden and unknown, looking down on the place where he had passed all his life. It was as if he were spying on himself and he stared in a trance of revulsion, all the details of his years of bitterness thronging before him. The evening after evening spent in the hotel, followed by the slow walk back to the house. The long hours of a Sunday . . . the silence, the rejection, the covered aggression . . . Murdo dropped his forehead on to the soft earth and bit at his thumb.

When the last layer of daylight had been pressed down into the sea out beyond the mouth of the loch and the street was only dimly seen beneath its two high lamps, Murdo waited to see the lights go on in the manse. But though the minutes passed, no sign of life appeared there.

It began to rain. He put on his hat and turned up the

collar of his coat and went on waiting with his hope now starting to waver. Later, when the first drinkers left the hotel and Murdo felt the last remnants of his patience succumbing to the cold and rain, he came out from the gorse and crept slowly down the hill.

It must have been about ten o'clock as he stood in the shadow of the great beech tree between the kirk and the hotel that the bar door opened and his old drinking companion, Donnie MacGillivray, came out and stood for a moment under the light, looking at the rain. He was a thin, lanky man with grizzled hair and grey, sparkling eyes with a lifelong love of the drink and a habit of ceaselessly licking his lips as he spoke. He walked unsteadily out of the light and into the rain.

'Donnie!'

'Eh? Who's that then?'

Murdo stepped forward to the edge of the light and beckoned the old man towards him.

'Murdo! Where in heaven's name have you been all this time? By Christ, I'd near on given you up for dead. Och and you look terrible! Here, have a drink.'

He produced the remains of a half-bottle from his pocket and offered it to Murdo. Murdo took it and tilted it back.

'Well, man? Where've you been?'

'Och, just away,' replied Murdo evasively. 'What like is the house?'

'Your house . . .?' Donnie looked away for a moment. 'It's fair badly damaged, Murdo.'

Murdo looked down and kicked at the grit for a moment before he spoke again.

'And Margaret's away, is she not?'

'Aye . . . David Melville was telling me she'd gone to her sister. Here, have another go.'

So they stood together under the tree with the rain pouring down and finished the bottle.

'Oh, this bloody rain! Here, Murdo, have you a place for the night or will you come back with me? It's no night to be out.'

'No, no thanks. I'm fine, Donnie. I've a few things to do.'

'Oh aye . . . Well, will I see you in the hotel tomorrow then?'

'Aye. I'll be there.'

'Right then, Murdo. Cheerio the now.'

'Cheerio.'

And so the tall man, walking away into the darkness, left Murdo beneath the tree while the rain beat down noisily on the tarmac.

CHAPTER ELEVEN

The rain redoubled its strength, sending great gouts of water down through the foliage of the beech tree, churning up the silt in the ditch into a guggling stream of mud and dead leaves and maintaining a ceaseless battering on the tarmac of the roadway.

Murdo looked up at the sky. Only in the glare of the street lamp could the grainy lengths of the rain be seen; elsewhere there was nothing but the blinding darkness and the sound of water. He blinked and wiped his face with the palm of his good hand. The other one was now so swollen and stiff that he could scarcely move it. A sudden dizziness filled his head and he leant against the tree and closed his eyes.

It was some time since Donnie had left him and Murdo, having continued to watch the manse in vain, had at last decided that he would have to wait till the morning to see the minister. Wherever the man was, he would be back to take the Sunday service. Now Murdo wondered if he should go to his house for the night: there was bound to be some part of it left intact where he could get out of the rain and sleep . . . Though the dizziness had passed, he felt that he was on the brink of collapse. For a moment, his pride buckled as he thought of taking up Donnie's offer of a bed for the night. But it was only a momentary weakness and was dismissed as some last stirring of strength told him to stand alone and to depend on nobody.

When the last people had gone home from the hotel and the light above the bar door went out, Murdo left the shadow of the tree and, passing under the lamp, vanished up the road. Here he turned off on to the ground which lay behind the village street. It was pitch dark and, though he knew the lie of the land well enough, he stumbled about among the tussocks and rocks in his exhaustion. On his left, standing out against the light of the street lamps, the little row of houses stood bulked against the light.

Suddenly, his leg caught in a knot of brackens and he went sprawling forwards. He landed with all his weight on his purulent hand and let out a throttled yell of pain. Pinned down by his agony, he lay rolling in the mud, half blubbering in his attempt to stifle the sounds which rose out of him against his will. He wanted to shout, to curse whatever it was that was so relentlessly crushing the strength from him. But as the first shock sank away, he simply lay there under the torrent of rain, mumbling senselessly.

His capacity for suffering seemed to have been finally exhausted. His pride was broken. All sense of bitterness and anger against the world's denial to him of what he had believed to be his due in life had ultimately been driven out. And so, unwillingly perhaps but nonetheless surely, he had reached his strange destination. Lying in the mud under the darkness, only a short way from the ruins of his home, Murdo Munro had found the answer for which he had been unwittingly waiting most of his life. Nearby, people talked softly and then fell asleep; all around, the whole northern world was resting in preparation for the struggles of the coming day; while he lay unknown, a mere nothing under the undimensioned and spreading night.

At long last, he got to his feet. As he walked the small distance to his house, he fell twice more but seemed to feel neither exasperation nor pain. He stood at the back of the building and saw all one half of its roof naked, a cross-pattern of roof-timbers against the light beyond. His eyes were glazed and dull. He let himself in at the back door and crunched across the remains of the kitchen into the sitting room.

There was nothing but the bare framework of the windows left and through the gaping hole, the light from the street cast a still paleness across the room. On what remained of the floor, bits and pieces of the heavier furniture, blackened wood held together by metal braces, lay about among the mess of wrinkled plastic, tattered material and broken glass. The stonework of the walls stood exposed though here and there patches of crumbling plaster held doggedly to the surface. Most of the ceiling had been burnt away and joists and smaller struts poked downwards, giving the room a cramped, barred appearance. The rain lay in puddles on the floor.

Murdo stood open-eyed before the scene of his destruction for a moment and then walked across the room. As he went, he felt a tightness bunching up inside him. He stopped, not understanding, as his body was swiftly taken hold of by the swelling pressure. His breath came in small, wheezy gasps. A second later, his face buckled as a blow struck him in the chest and a great claw seized his heart. With his knees folding beneath him, he staggered forward a step, saw a flashing image of the sun burning on the crest of a wave and then fell. With a dull, sickly sound, his head struck against a bracket of heavy metal. Knocked aside by the blow, he slumped forwards through the frame of the window. He lay motionless with his flap-eared head resting on the cold, wet slab of the sill while the rain washed the flow of blood across his face in a delicate network.

Murdo Munro was dead.

The people of Acheninver slept soundly in their homes. The rain continued until the last hours of the night when it thinned and then stopped as the clouds passed away over the island, leaving the darkness clear and still. As the hours went by, the sky began to reflect the first touches of the light that rose across the edge of distant horizons. Its waves drove in under the night sky and resolutely levered the darkness up and away from the eastern hills. Slowly at first but seeming ever to gather speed, it pressed upwards, its whitening light bluffly knocking the stars out of the sky and touching off the first signs of activity among the animals on the land below. For a long while yet, the night lay thick in the hills and glens but its blackness changed to purple and then dark blue as the sky overhead grew steadily brighter.

And then, with a sudden rush, the sun cast off from the mountains far to the east and began to creep up behind the island heights. Its first shafts of light pierced the passes and struck out over the village where the shadows were retreating below the hill. The shafts multiplied and slowly wheeled downwards to catch the uppermost crags of Beinn an Eòin beyond the head of the loch. As the minutes passed, the sunlight came on down across the slopes below the rocks and advanced out into the glen. And, at last, with a brilliance of light and power, the sun rose a little higher and was shining down on the village. The sky was white and blue and yellow; the tide was flooding in the loch; everything was bright with water and light. Up on Beinn an Eòin, a lone buzzard turned sleepily on the back of a breeze.

An hour later, Walter MacFarlane stood shaving in the bathroom of the manse. As he pushed his head back and shaved under his chin, he thought over the meeting he had attended in the town the evening before. Then, having rinsed the razor, he gazed out of the window and thought to himself that a man was indeed lucky to be alive on such a Sunday morning.

Down at the other end of the village street, a door

opened and two little girls came quietly out and, whispering to each other, went past the burnt house and along to a patch of grass behind the shop and began to play.

A while later, with the village still quiet under the dazzling sunlight, a collared turtle dove fluttered down and landed on the gutter of the charred roof. It cooed rhythmically for a few minutes and then, falling silent, looked from side to side as if in amazement.